"I'd like to kiss you at midnight. If that's all right with you."

He was actually asking if it was all right to kiss her on New Year's Eve?

Someone in the crowd began the traditional countdown....

"Ten, nine, eight—"

"And you are?" Jorge asked.

"Seven, six, five—"

"Jane Gilliam."

"Four, three—"

Was it his imagination, or was there a new spark in her eyes? She was definitely arousing him.

"Two—"

He drew her into his arms.

"You're not really going to kiss me, are you?" Dream or not, it was still hard to believe. And yet she *so* wanted to believe.

"One!"

His lips covered hers as cries of "Happy New ~~Year!~~" ~~rang~~ ~~through the crow~~ded room.

~~...~~ ~~...~~ other than the

Dear Reader,

Welcome to the latest miniseries about the Fortunes, the family that seems to have more than its share of money, adventures and drama. This first book reintroduces you to the family via the very sexy, very commitment-phobic family friend Jorge Mendoza. Once a rancher, now a charismatic entrepreneur, the ever-sexy Jorge never lacks for female companionship. That he is alone tonight is by choice. And Fate. Because tonight his path will cross that of Jane Gilliam, a lovely, down-to-earth young woman who is at the party hosted by the head of the Fortune Foundation and held at Jorge's parents' restaurant, Red. It wasn't her intention to be there in order to meet the man of her dreams, her ultimate partner for eternity. But Fate had another idea for both these people. Read on and find out what it is.

As ever, I thank you for reading and I wish you someone to love who loves you back.

Love,

Marie Ferrarella

MARIE FERRARELLA

PLAIN JANE AND THE PLAYBOY

SPECIAL EDITION®

Published by Silhouette Books

America's Publisher of Contemporary Romance

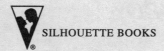 SILHOUETTE BOOKS

ISBN-13: 978-0-373-65428-4
ISBN-10:   0-373-65428-6

Recycling programs
for this product may
not exist in your area.

PLAIN JANE AND THE PLAYBOY

Copyright © 2009 by Marie Rydzynski-Ferrarella

Visit Silhouette Books at www.eHarlequin.com

Printed in U.S.A.

Books by Marie Ferrarella

MARIE FERRARELLA

This *USA TODAY* bestselling and RITA® Award-winning author has written over one hundred and fifty novels for Silhouette Books, some under the name Marie Nicole. Her romances are beloved by fans worldwide. Visit her Web site at www.marieferrarella.com.

To
Margaret Watson,
for reams of e-mail
and priceless
support.
Thank you.

Chapter One

Red, the extremely popular restaurant located in Red Rock, Texas, and the realization of a dream by José and Maria Mendoza, had closed its doors to the public this holiday evening.

But it was far from empty. The premises had been rented out to Emmett Jamison who, along with his wife, Linda, both former FBI agents, oversaw the Fortune Foundation, a philanthropic organization now in its fourth year. The guests at the New Year's Eve party included key personnel at the foundation, as well as every single member of the Fortune family who could walk or crawl within a fifty-mile radius.

Included, too, were a large number of friends, not the least of whom were more than several members of the Mendoza family. There were so many people packed inside the converted former hacienda—said to have once belonged to distant relatives of Santa Ana—that guests were spilling out onto the inner courtyard, despite the cold temperature. The press of bodies generated its own heat.

Good cheer abounded, mixing with the occasional strains of festive music, some of it coming from the old-fashioned jukebox, some of it from the five-piece band that Maria had hired at her son, Jorge's behest. Christmas carols meshed with both Mexican and country music. It was a veritable potpourri of everything that Texas stood for.

Almost everyone seemed to be having a good time, if noise could be considered a barometer of fun. The only true difficulty was in maneuvering through the throng, and in locating people the crowd had swallowed up.

So when Jack Fortune all but walked into his brother-in-law as Jorge finished placing a fruity, mixed drink on a comely young woman's table, he took advantage of the situation.

Hooking his arm around his brother-in-law's neck, Jack said playfully, "Hey, there's a vicious rumor making the rounds that Jorge Mendoza is actually here without a date." Hearing Jack's voice, Jorge relaxed, lowering the tray he was about to use as a weapon. "I've been defending your reputation," Jack continued, releasing his hold on Jorge, "saying that it just wasn't possible, this being New Year's Eve and all."

"I'm afraid that you've been wasting your breath, Jack," Jorge said, turning around to face the man who made his sister Gloria's world spin on its axis. Out of the corner of his eye, he saw Gloria making her way toward them. "The rumor's true. I didn't bring anyone to the party."

There was a very good reason for that, but Jorge kept it to himself. The current lady in his life, Edie, was hinting broadly about their relationship. She wanted an honest-to-gosh commitment from him, even though they'd only been seeing each other for about a month. And while it had been a very enjoyable month, with several memorable moments, none of it was earthshaking enough to prompt him to make the relationship permanent.

He felt sure that neglecting to invite her to share New Year's Eve would send her a message about his intentions. So he'd opted to go it alone tonight, thereby dodging a very real bullet with his name on it.

"Is it terminal?" Jack asked.

Confused, wondering if he'd misheard, Jorge leaned forward. "Is what terminal?"

"Your illness," Jack answered. "You're sick, right? That's got to be the reason you didn't bring anyone. I've never known you to be without female companionship for more than, what? Fifteen minutes at a time?" Jorge went through women the way his father, José, went through clean undershirts in a hot kitchen. "Legend has it you tried to pick up a candy striper in the nursery the day you were born."

Jorge laughed, shaking his dark head, his deep brown eyes crinkling. "I'm not sick, Jack. I thought I'd just help Mom and Dad out tonight. You know, wait on tables, tend bar, mix drinks—"

"Flirt with every woman under the age of a hundred," Gloria interjected, completing her older brother's sentence as she came up to join him and her husband. She hooked her arm through Jack's, but her attention was clearly on Jorge.

"Right." Jorge saw no reason to deny that charge. He believed in enjoying himself whenever he could. And flirting was his inalienable right. Flashing his thousand-watt smile, he repeated, "But I'm only here to help out. Besides," he confided, "if I brought someone with me to this little fiesta, Mom would immediately think it was serious. You know what she's like." In her time Maria Mendoza had been on each of his now-married sisters' cases. "She'd be writing out wedding invitations right after the stroke of midnight." He considered that, then amended, "Maybe even before."

"Mom just wants you to be happy, big brother," Christina chimed in, coming in at the tail end of the conversation, her fingers firmly laced through her husband Derek's. It took a little maneuvering to join the threesome.

Jorge gave Christina a lecherous wink. "Mom and I have a *very* different definition of happiness."

"I'll say," Sierra agreed sarcastically, as she and her husband, Alex, came up to join the other two couples and Jorge in the impromptu family meeting.

"Mom wants to see you married with a family and you just want to go from woman to woman, gathering honey like a drunken bee going from flower to flower."

Jorge rolled his eyes. "A *happy* drunken bee," he emphasized.

Gloria rolled her eyes. There was no changing a leopard's spots and it seemed that there was no changing Jorge. He was going to be a playboy until the day he died.

"You're hopeless," she told him with a sigh.

Again, he saw no reason to deny the truth. He was what he was—a man who loved women. And from where he stood, there were so many women out there to love.

"Exactly," Jorge responded, the same killer, boyish grin that had made many women weak in the knees gracing his lips. He leaned into Gloria, as if to impart something confidential. "I'd give up trying to change me if I were you. Now go dance with your husband, Glory," he urged, then turned to his two other sisters. "You, too, Sierra, Christina. Don't harass the help. I have drinks to make and pretty women to wait on," Jorge told them just before he turned away and faded into the crowd as he headed back to the bar.

Gloria shook her head. A sigh escaped her lips. "There goes one unhappy man."

Jack took Gloria by the hand, deciding that his brother-in-law had a good idea. He pressed his hand against the small of her back and slowly began to sway in time to the music. "Oh, I don't know. He didn't seem all that unhappy to me."

Men could be so dense, Gloria thought, seeing only what was on the surface and nothing more. "Ever hear of the expression, laughing on the outside, crying on the inside?"

This was not an argument he was about to win, Jack thought, and he was far too shrewd a businessman to continue fighting a doomed battle. Especially not on New Year's Eve.

"You're absolutely right," he told Gloria solemnly. "Jorge's a very unhappy man."

Gloria knew sarcasm even when it was disguised as surrender, but she didn't want to fight. She did, however, want some kind of solution. She wanted Jorge to be as happy as she was. She'd found marriage far preferable to the single life—as long as it was to the right person.

"Can you come up with someone for him?" Gloria asked suddenly as he swung her around in the little bit of space he'd staked out for them.

"Then I'd be the unhappy man," Jack pointed out. Gloria looked at him, puzzled. "You know Jorge doesn't like us interfering in his life."

None of them liked people butting into their lives, but sometimes, it was just necessary. For their own good. "I just don't like seeing him so alone, Jack."

Jack glanced over his shoulder. Jorge was behind the bar again, mixing drinks and talking to a well-endowed young blonde who seemed to be hanging on his every word. And having a great deal of difficulty remaining in her dress.

"Trust me, Glory. Jorge is never alone for more than four minutes at a time. Five, tops."

Gloria looked at her brother. She had an entirely different take on the scene. The woman was a bimbo. Happily-ever-after didn't happen with bimbos.

"Men," Gloria huffed.

Jack smiled broadly in response. "Glad you noticed that." His eyes gleamed as he looked at his wife. She was every bit as gorgeous, as sexy, as the day he'd fallen in love with her. "What do you say, right after midnight, we—" Jack leaned in and whispered the rest of his thought into her ear.

Gloria's eyes widened and then her lips curved in deep appreciation. Thoughts and concerns about Jorge and his lifestyle were temporarily placed on the back burner. The far back burner.

"You're on," she told her husband.

Pleased by her response, Jack continued dancing with his wife.

Maria Mendoza paused and momentarily stopped worrying if there was enough food to keep this crowd well fed, and just took in the happy revelers. Moving back, she found herself, quite by accident, bumping into Patrick Fortune, the retired president of Fortune-Rockwell and father of five of the people here. More importantly, a good friend for several decades.

"Your son is making my daughter very happy,"

she said to Patrick the moment he was within earshot. Patrick had been the one she'd turned to several years ago, enlisting his help to find a suitable husband for Gloria, her once very troubled daughter.

Maternal pleasure now radiated from every pore as Maria spoke to the tall, distinguished, redheaded man at her side.

Patrick silently lifted his glass of white wine in the general direction of his son and daughter-in-law. He was as pleased by the union as Maria was. It was nice to see Jack happy for a change.

"That did turn out rather well, didn't it?" he said proudly.

"And it was all your doing," Maria reminded him, more than willing to give credit where it was due.

Ever modest, Patrick didn't quite see it that way. "All I did was call him home to help Gloria get her new jewelry business on its feet. Chemistry did the rest."

"Chemistry," Maria allowed with a slight nod of her head. "And a lot of lit candles and prayers to the Blessed Virgin," she added with more enthusiasm. And then she sighed, thinking of her two sons. "But no amount of prayers seem to be working when it comes to Jorge—or Roberto for that matter." Both represented two rather sore spots in her very large heart. "Roberto didn't even think enough of the family to come home for the holidays." He lived in Denver now, so very far away. She'd called her first-born twice, only to get an annoying answering machine both times.

And no return call.

Patrick knew how hurtful that could be. "The boy's busy, Maria," he told her gently.

"Boy," she echoed the term her friend had used. "He's my eldest. How can Roberto be a boy when he's forty years old?"

She knew better than that, Patrick thought. "Because, to us, no matter what their age, they will always be our children. Our boys and girls." Finished with his wine, he set the glass down on an empty table. "Which is why you worry, Maria," Patrick pointed out. Good humor highlighted his aristocratic features. "Stop worrying," he advised. "Things will turn out all right in the end. You did a good job raising them. They're good people. All of them. Once in a while, it takes a little extra time for them to find their way," he told her. "But they always do in the end." He smiled encouragingly at her. "You just have to have faith."

Maria sighed. He really believed that, she thought. "You truly are an amazing man."

Taking Maria's hand in his, he gave it a gentle squeeze. "Don't worry," he repeated. "And if it makes you feel any better," he added, "I'll look around and see if there's anyone suitable to put in Jorge's path."

"Thank you, old friend," Maria replied with enthusiasm.

"Maria," a deep male voice called out just then, slicing through the noise. "*Ven aca.* I need you." The blend of Spanish and English had an urgency to it. Maria turned to see her husband, José, waving to her, beckoning her toward the kitchen. "We are running out of your special tacquitos."

"Coming, my love," she called back. Saying "thank you" one more time to Patrick, the petite woman burrowed her way through the crowd of people to reach her husband.

Patrick Fortune remained where he was, watching the object of his old friend's concern a moment longer.

The last thing that Jorge Mendoza resembled was a troubled, lonely young man, he thought. Even though he claimed to be working, Jorge, ensconced behind the bar now, appeared to be having the time of his life. He was moving from one young woman to another, seemingly taking orders for drinks and lingering to flirt, most likely mentally compiling yet another list of names and accompanying phone numbers. The young man was a modern-day Casanova, clearly enjoying both his freedom and the hunt.

Eventually though, Patrick was convinced that Maria Mendoza's wayward son would realize that "freedom" and the hunt were definitely not nearly as important as the love of a good woman—the *right* good woman. And he was a romantic, Patrick thought. He believed that there was someone for everyone. There certainly had been for him.

"Looks like the family's out in full force," Jack commented, coming up beside his father, Emmett Jamison at his side. Gloria was a few feet away, talking to Emmett's wife, Linda, about a necklace Linda wanted fashioned.

"Most of them," Patrick corrected. Although his sister Cynthia's children were here, Cynthia was conspicuously absent, despite the invitation to attend. It looked as if the estrangement between them was going to go on a little longer, he thought. "Look, I wanted to run something by you, Emmett."

"Business, Dad?" Jack asked. "I thought you were the one who finally said all work and no play—"

"This is about family," he explained to Jack, then turned back to Emmett. "Nothing worse than having your own son preach at you, especially when he's throwing your own words back at you," Patrick told Emmett. "I was hoping you might find positions at the Foundation for several of my brother William's kids. It might help bring the rest of the clan closer together."

Emmett nodded, always open to anything the older man had to say. "I'll see what I can do."

Patrick patted him on the shoulder. "Can't ask for anything more than that."

Patrick Fortune and Jorge's sisters were not the only ones observing the playboy's progress from woman to willing woman. Jorge was also an object of awe for Emmett's adopted son, Ricky, who was nursing a very serious case of envy. Envy that encompassed both the charming Jorge and his best friend, Josh Fredericks. Josh was a suave seventeen and had a steady girlfriend, Lindsey, on his arm, while he, Ricky, was a very unsure-of-himself fourteen.

It seemed as if everyone here had someone but him—and that woman sitting over in the corner by herself, he noted. Jorge seemed to have not just one but a harem of women. Every single one who came up to the bar left with a smitten smile on her face.

How did he *do* that?

Working up his courage, Ricky finally made his way over to the bar, and Jorge. But when he reached the bar, all he could do was silently observe. Jorge was a master at work.

It took Jorge a few minutes to notice the teenager. Wiping the counter down in front of him, Jorge flashed a grin as he shook his head.

"Sorry, Ricky, afraid all I can offer you is a soda pop or a Virgin Mary." The boy looked at him a little uncertainly. "That's a Bloody Mary without the alcohol," Jorge explained, lowering his voice so as not to embarrass the boy.

Ricky shook his head. "Oh, no, no, I don't want anything to drink," he protested, stuttering a little. Tongue-tied, he got no further.

Jorge threw the damp towel behind the bar and leaned forward, creating an aura of privacy despite the crowd. The boy looked like he wanted to talk, but didn't know how to start. Jorge felt sorry for him. "Then what is it I can do for you?"

Ricky felt more uncertain than ever, more awkward than he had in a very long time. But it was now or never. Clearing his throat nervously, he looked around to make sure that no one in the area was listening.

"I want to know how you do it," he finally said.

But Jorge couldn't hear him. "What?"

Ricky repeated himself, this time a little more audibly. "I want to know how you do it."

Obviously hearing did not bring enlightenment with it. "Do what?"

This was going to be harder than he thought. Ricky licked his lower lip, which had suddenly grown even drier than his upper one had.

"How do you get all these ladies to flirt with you?" he blurted out. "I've been watching you work all night and there had to have been at least twenty of them." Old and young, they all seemed to bloom in Jorge's presence.

"Twenty-six," Jorge corrected with a quick conspiratorial wink, then said simply, "They're thirsty."

"They're not coming over to the bar for the drinks," Ricky protested. He might not be a smooth operator, like Jorge, but he was bright enough to see that ordering a drink was just an excuse, not a reason. "They're coming to talk to you." He paused to work up his flagging courage. "How do I do that?" he wanted to know. "How do I get them to come to me?" And then he added more realistically, "Or, at least, get them not to run off when I come to them."

Jorge laughed gently, taking care not to sound as if he was laughing at the boy. He'd never had that problem himself. Women had always come on to him, even before he discovered the fine art of flirtation. But he could feel sympathy for the boy who seemed so painfully shy. "They don't run off from you, Ricky."

Ricky knew the difference between truth and flattery. "Yes, they do. I asked a girl in my class to come with me tonight and she said she couldn't. She said—" He paused for a second, working his way past the embarrassment. "She said her mother wouldn't let her stay out that late."

It was a plausible enough excuse, Jorge thought, although the girls he'd known at Ricky's age had bent rules, ignored parental limitations and come shinning down trees growing next to their bedroom windows just to see him for a few stolen hours.

"How old are you again, Ricky?"

The boy unconsciously squared his rather thin shoulders before answering. "Fourteen."

"Fourteen," Jorge repeated thoughtfully. "Well, she was probably telling the truth, then." He did his best to appear somber. "When my sisters were each fourteen, my father would have chained them in the stable to keep them from going out with a boy, much less staying out until midnight."

That didn't seem like a good enough excuse to assuage his ego. "But it's New Year's Eve. Besides, times have changed," Ricky pointed out.

The boy had a lot to learn, Jorge thought. "Parents haven't," he assured the boy. "And, if you want some advice—"

Ricky's eyes widened and all but gleamed. "Please," he encouraged enthusiastically.

"First, you have to have confidence in yourself." He saw the disappointed, skeptical look that entered the boy's eyes. Expecting the secret of the ages, he was receiving an advice column platitude. "You can do it," Jorge continued. "No girl is going to want to go out with you if you act like you don't want to be around yourself. Understand?"

A little of Ricky's disappointment abated. "I think so."

Jorge nodded. Since no one was approaching the bar at the moment, he decided to be more generous with his advice. "And this next point is the most important thing you'll ever learn about dealing with a woman."

"What?" Ricky asked breathlessly, Ponce DeLeon about to uncover the fountain of youth.

Jorge lowered his voice. "When talking to a girl, always make her feel as if she's the prettiest girl in the room."

Ricky swallowed and glanced over at Lizzie Fortune, the girl who made the very air back up in his lungs. Lizzie was a distant Fortune cousin, just in town for the holidays. His heart had melted the moment he laid eyes on her this evening.

He didn't have a snowball's chance in hell with someone who looked like that. And he doubted that Jorge's magic formula would have any effect on Lizzie.

"What if she already *is* the prettiest girl in the room?" he wanted to know.

"Then it's even easier," Jorge told him. "You can handle any girl. Just have confidence in yourself, Ricky, and the rest will be a piece of cake."

Ricky was still more than a little uncertain. Just breathing was enough for someone who looked like

Jorge. But for someone like him, it wasn't that simple. "And this always works?"

"Always," Jorge said confidently.

But he could see that Ricky still had his doubts. The boy definitely needed a demonstration, Jorge decided. "Tell you what," he proposed. "You pick any girl in this room and I'll have her eating out of my hand in no time."

Ricky's eyes widened far enough to fall out. "Any girl?"

"Any girl," Jorge agreed. "Just make sure she's not married. We don't want to start any fights here in my parents' restaurant."

Ricky was perfectly amendable to that. "Okay," he agreed, bobbing his head up and down. He was already scanning the crowded room for a candidate.

Ricky stopped looking when his line of vision returned to the woman he'd spotted earlier, sitting by herself at a table. There was a frown on her face as she regarded her half-empty glass and she was very obviously alone. It was a table for two and there was no indication that anyone had recently vacated the other chair.

There was even a book on the table in front of her. Was she reading? Whether she was or not, there seemed to be an air of melancholy about her, visible even at this distance.

"Her," Ricky announced, pointing to the woman. "I pick her."

Chapter Two

Rising to the challenge, Jorge attempted to focus in the general direction that Ricky indicated.

The woman was clearly the stereotypical wallflower. She was sitting at the corner table all by herself, twirling a lock of long curly brown hair around her finger, the festive lights shimmering off her shiny green dress.

"Hey, man, I don't want to get arrested just to prove a point," Jorge protested. When Ricky looked at him quizzically, Jorge added, "She looks like a kid."

Ricky shook his head. "She's not. I heard her talking to someone earlier. She works for some kids' literacy foundation, tutoring them and sometimes holding fund-raisers to buy extra books. I think it's called Red Rock ReadingWorks," Ricky volunteered. He looked at Jorge expectantly. "She's gotta be at least twenty."

Jorge grinned at the boy's tone. He was thirty-eight himself, but he doubted Ricky knew that. "Then she's ancient, huh?"

"Hey, I'm fourteen. Everybody's ancient to me." Feeling as if he'd just put one foot in his mouth, Ricky quickly added, "Except you, of course."

Jorge's grin widened. "Nice save," he commented.

Ricky glanced back toward the girl at the table before looking up at his hero again. Jorge hadn't made a move yet.

"Backing down?" he wanted to know.

Nothing he liked better than a challenge, although, given his experience, the young woman at the table didn't look as if she'd put up much resistance.

"Not a chance," Jorge told him. He looked around and then saw one of the restaurant's employees at the far end of the bar. Perfect. "Hey, Angel," he called over the din. The man looked in his direction and raised a brow. "Mind taking over for me for a few minutes? I haven't had a break all night."

Jorge was the owners' son and what he wanted, he would have gotten without question even if he wasn't so affable. Angel nodded and came around to the other side of the bar.

"No problem."

Untying the half black apron secured around his slim waist, Jorge surrendered it to Angel. He felt invigorated. He was back in hunting mode.

Jane Gilliam had really hoped that coming to the party tonight would help her shake off the dark mood that had all but enshrouded her these last few days. Three days to be exact.

Three days since Eddie Gibbs had unceremoniously, and without prior warning, dumped her.

She probably wouldn't have even known she was being dumped, at least not for a few more days, if it wasn't for New Year's Eve. She'd impulsively asked the man she'd been seeing for the last six months to this New Year's Eve extravaganza that her close friend, Isabella Mendoza, had invited her to.

Eddie had listened to her impatiently and then he'd turned her down. She hadn't been prepared for that and when she'd asked him why, Eddie had bluntly told her that he would be spending New Year's Eve with someone else.

With his new girlfriend.

Jane could feel the sting of tears starting again and she passed her hand over her eyes, wiping them away. Up until that point, she'd thought that *she* was Eddie's girlfriend. But somewhere along the line in the last month, a month in which Eddie had been making himself increasingly scarce, he had decided that he "could do better"—his very words, each tipped in heart-piercing titanium—and found himself someone else.

The only trouble with that was that he'd forgotten to tell *her*.

Jane let out a long, shaky breath. She supposed she should have seen it coming. After all, it wasn't as if she was a knockout. And cute guys like Eddie Gibbs didn't stay with mousy girls like her, at least not for long.

Women, Jane silently corrected herself. *Women.* She was twenty-five years old. At twenty-five, you weren't a girl anymore; you were a woman.

A very lonely woman, Jane thought glumly, looking into the bottom of her glass. The drink had long since become watered down, the ice cubes melting into what had once been a fruity piña colada. It had turned the liquid into an exceedingly pale shade of yellow.

She needed to get out of here, she told herself. At this point, she didn't know what she could have been thinking, agreeing to come here with Isabella. Seeing all these couples, whispering into each other's ear, clearly enjoying themselves, was just making her feel more hopeless.

More alone.

Besides, it was getting pretty close to midnight, when the New Year was ushered in with heartfelt, soulful, passionate kisses. Seeing all these couples wrapped in each other's arms, kissing in the New Year was much more than she was going to be able to stand.

Up until three days ago, she thought she'd be kissing Eddie at the stroke of midnight. Now, she thought dejectedly, she'd probably be the only one here who had no one to turn to as the glittering silver ball on the wide-screen, flat-panel television reached the bottom of the pole and sent off an array of wild, blinding sparklers to greet the incoming year.

She didn't need to see that.

Didn't need to feel like a loser.

Again.

Jane glanced at her watch. Less than ten minutes left before midnight. That didn't give her much time to make her escape.

As if anyone would notice her leaving, she thought mockingly. She'd come here with Isabella, but there had to be a taxicab out there somewhere, didn't there? This was a big night for inebriated people. Cab drivers made their money on nights like New Year's Eve.

"Freshen that up for you?" asked a deep, melodic voice directly above her.

Jane realized that the voice—and the question— belonged to one of the waiters. He was obviously asking about the drink she'd been pretending to nurse for the last two hours. She'd already set the glass aside. The colorful little umbrella was drooping badly, mirroring the way she felt inside.

"No," she replied politely, "I was just…"

The rest of her thought vanished, as did, just for a moment, her entire thinking process. All because she'd made the mistake of looking up at the owner of the low, rumbling, sexy voice.

The man who had asked the question was, in a

word, beautiful. Not just handsome—although he was quite possibly the handsomest man, up close or on the movie screen, that she had ever seen in her life—but actually teeth-jarringly heart-stoppingly beautiful.

He had soulful brown eyes that she could have gotten lost in for at least the next ten years, and straight black hair that was just a little on the long side. Tall, lean, muscular, with jeans that emphasized his slender hips—and every move he made—whoever this man was, he made her think of a young lion.

On the other hand, his smile made her think of nothing at all, because just seeing it effectively turned her very intelligent and active brain to the consistency of last week's mush.

Struggling to collect herself and retrieve whatever might still be left of her composure, Jane did her best not to sound as if she was currently understudying the part of the head idiot of a very large village.

"Excuse me?"

"Your drink," Jorge prodded, nodding at the glass next to her elbow on the table. "May I freshen it up for you?" Lifting it to his nose, he took a sniff. "Piña colada, right?" he guessed. And then, when she said nothing at all, he smiled again, completing the transformation of the organ that was in her chest from a functioning heart to a puddle of red liquid. "My parents have me tending the bar," he explained, "and making sure that lovely ladies like you don't have to wait too long to have their requests granted."

Lovely ladies. How could someone so beautiful be so blind? she wondered. She wasn't lovely, she was plain and she knew it.

The ball on the TV panel on the back wall looked as if it was going to begin its descent at any moment.

Get out of here, her survival streak ordered urgently.

Coming to, Jane shook her head. "No, that's all right," she told him as he reached for her glass. "I was just about to leave anyway."

He looked at her in surprise. "Leave? Before midnight?" He made it sound as if she were doing something revolutionary.

Jane lifted her shoulders in a vague shrug. The left strap of her dress slipped off, sliding down her upper arm.

Jorge, his eyes on hers, reached out and very slowly slid the strap back into place.

Jane felt as if her skin had just caught on fire. She was rather surprised that she didn't actually spontaneously combust. The puddle in the middle of her chest became a heart again and instantly went into triple time, hammering so hard she was having trouble just catching her breath.

"Doesn't seem to be much point in staying," she heard herself saying, although she wasn't conscious of forming the words.

"And why is that?" he asked gently.

Just the sound of his voice made her feel warm all over. It took her a moment to realize that he'd asked her a question and another moment to focus on the words, making sense out of them.

"People always kiss someone at the stroke of midnight on New Year's Eve…"

Not sure how to end this sentence without sounding like a loser, Jane just let her voice trail off, hoping he'd silently fill in the rest of it himself. And have the decency to leave.

"And you have no one to kiss?" Jorge asked incredulously. His eyes swept over her. She could almost feel them. "A pretty lady like you?"

Jane could feel heat traveling up her cheeks and down her throat until all of her felt as if it were glowing pink.

"I just broke up with someone," she finally told him.

Breaking up sounded a great deal better than saying she'd just been dumped, Jane thought. But even so, the lie weighed heavily on her tongue. She didn't like lies, no matter what the reason, and here she was, hiding behind one so that she didn't come across like the ultimate loser to a man she didn't even know.

"His loss."

The man said it with such sincerity she found herself believing him, even though there was no way he could have meant that. After all, they were strangers to one another. For all he knew, she was a shrew.

Jane picked up her purse, holding it to her chest. "Well, I doubt if he thinks so. He's already found someone else."

What made her say that? a little voice in her head demanded. Why was she always so hell-bent on the truth, on making herself seem like she wasn't worthy of a committed relationship? The kids she worked with at the foundation loved her. Their parents were all grateful to her, praising her for making such a difference in the children's lives. And she got along rather well with the people she worked with at ReadingWorks, as long as the parameters remained in place—she was a colleague. A professional. Her personal life—such as it was—stayed private.

"Then he's a fool," Jorge told her quietly. "And you're better off without him."

As he spoke, Jorge studied the woman before him. It was one of his favorite pastimes. Every woman, he'd come to discover at a very early age, had something that was attractive about her. Something special, no matter how small.

This one, he thought, was actually pretty, in a plain sort of way. And by that, he meant that she was pretty without having to resort to artfully applied makeup, like so many of the other women who were here tonight. She was slender, petite—he doubted if she could have been more than about five two—and she had beautiful hair held in place with two ornamental hairclips. They allowed her golden brown curls to cascade down her back like a waterfall.

But what really captivated him was her innocence. There was a certain sweetness to her, a vulnerability that he now detected in her eyes. He sincerely doubted that she was aware of it.

But he was.

Jane stood up. It was almost midnight and she

really didn't want to feel like the odd woman out, not tonight. It would hurt too much.

But as she rose to her feet, the tall, beautiful young man with the sexy, velvet voice didn't retreat, didn't even take a step back. He remained exactly where he was, leaving less than a ribbon's worth of space between them.

So little space that she could actually feel the heat of his body radiating out to hers. Or was that just her body getting ready to burst into flame?

She swallowed. Why was he standing in her way? Was he laughing at her?

But he didn't seem as if he was laughing. His smile was too gentle, too kind.

Jane took a breath. "I really need to leave," she told him.

He slowly ran the back of his hand along her bare arm. "Would you stay if there was someone to kiss at the stroke of midnight?"

Goose bumps were forming on her arm at a fantastic rate. Her throat felt suddenly very, very dry.

Idiot, he's not saying what you think he's saying. He's just asking a question. Don't set yourself up to be a pathetic loser. Again.

But despite her stern, silent warning, Jane heard herself answering, "Yes." And then, to save face, she tried to make light of the situation. "Are you planning on dragging someone over here to kiss me?"

Eyes the color of warm chocolate on a cold winter morning held hers prisoner.

"No," he told her quietly.

Okay, now she really did feel like an idiot. Served her right for trying to flirt, or whatever she'd just done that might have passed for flirting. She wasn't any good at that—never had been.

Doing her best to salvage what was left of her badly damaged ego, Jane forced a smile to her lips. But all she could manage was barely half of one.

"Well, then," she murmured, attempting to get past him. "I'd better get going."

"No," Jorge repeated. "I'm not going to drag anyone over here—I'd like to be the one to kiss you at midnight." And then he looked at her with just the right touch of shyness. "If that's all right with you."

He was actually asking if it was all right to kiss her on New Year's Eve?

Was this some kind of a joke? Men like—what was his name, anyway? Men like him didn't ask permission to kiss a woman, they spent half their time fighting off women who were trying to kiss them.

Jane took another deep breath and held it for a moment, wondering whether she was dreaming. What other explanation could there be? How in heaven's name didn't he already have a girlfriend in tow on this occasion? She would have been willing to bet, until this man with the magnetic smile had approached her, that she was quite probably the only unattached adult here.

"What's your name?" Jane finally asked him.

"Jorge," he replied. "Jorge Mendoza."

Mendoza.

It was certainly a common enough name. Even so, Jane couldn't help wondering if Jorge was somehow related to Isabella and if her friend had sent him here on an errand of mercy.

A mercy kissing.

Out of the corner of her eye, she took note of the TV screen. The glittering Times Square ball was definitely beginning to move downward now. Someone in the crowd raised his voice and began the traditional countdown, ticking off the seconds that were still left in this year.

"Ten, nine, eight—"

When the woman made no effort to identify herself, Jorge coaxed her a little. "And you are?"

Several voices joined in, more swelling their numbers with each passing second. "Seven, six, five—"

She wasn't a bold person by nature, but if this was a dream, then there was no reason to worry about consequences. Nothing to be embarrassed about in the future.

"Jane. Jane Gilliam," she told him. "Are you related to Isabella?"

"Four, three—"

"Cousin," he told her. Was it his imagination, or was there a new spark in her eyes? He found his interest being piqued and discovered that she was definitely arousing him. "Distant," he added for good measure.

"Two—"

Without any further discussion, his eyes on hers,

Jorge drew Jane into his arms. He could feel her breathing become audible and found something very sweet about the almost hesitant anticipation he saw in her eyes.

"You're not really going to kiss me, are you?" Dream or not, it was still hard for her to believe. And yet, she *so* wanted to believe.

"One!"

His lips covered hers as cries of "Happy New Year!" echoed throughout the crowded room, shouted from the announcer on the TV program as well as by the various people scattered about whose lips were not otherwise occupied.

But Jane didn't hear a single sound, other than the pounding of her heart.

Chapter Three

She'd died.

There was no other explanation for the way she felt, Jane thought. She must have died and zoomed straight up to heaven. And not even the regular heaven, but some higher plane reserved for the incredibly saintly, incredibly fortunate. Because there was nothing remotely earthly about the feelings she was experiencing right at this moment.

To the casual observer, Jane was certain that it looked as if like nothing more than a traditional New Year's Eve kiss was being shared by two people at the stroke of midnight.

A lot the casual observer knew.

There were fireworks exploding in her veins, not

to mention that her head was spinning wildly, threatening to throw her completely off balance and utterly out of control. Granted, her experience when it came to men and kissing was rather sadly limited, but even she knew that this was something unusual, something really and deliciously different. She'd never been on the verge of a complete meltdown before.

Jorge tasted incredibly sweet and he smelled even better. Everything about him aroused her.

Bold was a word that had nothing to do with her personality, outside of those times when she attempted to secure more funding for her nonprofit organization. But she felt bold now. Bold enough to press her enflamed body against Jorge's in an attempt to absorb every nuance, every fragment of this incredible experience that had taken her completely by surprise and swept her not just off her feet but off to another dimension.

Another universe.

Like a woman trapped in a mind-boggling, sensuous trance, Jane wove her arms around Jorge's neck, praying the dream she was having would never end. Praying that the moment she was in would stretch out until eternity. She'd never felt so alive, so wonderful before. And probably never would again.

He was rattled.

Few things ever rattled Jorge Mendoza. He was thirty-eight and eons away from being a boy, even though he still possessed not only a boyish grin, but boyish charm. Even in his teens, he'd been more man than boy, with a man's take on things. And heaven knew he'd kissed and been with more than twice his share of women.

Life had been good to him that way, he'd often thought, blessing him not just with exceptional looks but, more importantly, with a magnetic charm. Charm that now aided him in his professional endeavors—currently he was gathering financial backing for a trainer who raised the finest quarter horses in Texas—as well as in the seduction of willing women.

But none of that was on his mind right now. Instead, he felt complete and total, unabashed surprise. He hadn't thought that he could *ever* feel like this. Like there were rockets going off in his veins.

That kind of feeling hadn't happened to him since the first time he'd slept with a woman.

But this pretty, intelligent but obviously inexperienced young woman had just managed to do what no other woman had in the last twenty-four years. She'd jarred him down to his very foundations and made him feel like a boy on the brink of manhood again.

It was with incredible effort that Jorge managed to finally, albeit reluctantly, draw his lips away from Jane's.

Taking in a deep, steadying breath, he looked down at the young woman the way one might look at a soul-shaking revelation, attempting to analyze it. Very slowly, surprise gave way to abject pleasure.

"Happy New Year," he whispered softly against her hair.

"Right." She was rather stunned that she could actually talk rather than simply gasp. "Happy New Year," she repeated, each syllable accompanied by the mad beating of her heart. Hands down, this certainly was the best New Year's Eve moment she'd ever experienced.

His dark eyes danced, smiling directly into her soul. "So," he asked her, "what are you doing for the rest of the year?"

"Recovering."

The honest admission had just slipped out before Jane could think to stop it. But being coy was not something she had any practice at, or, truthfully, any desire to become proficient in. There'd always been something off-putting to her about women who felt the need to play games with the men in their lives.

By the same token, though, she'd discovered that since she didn't play games, it wasn't very long before she had no one to even contemplate playing games with. The few men who had passed through her life would come on strong and when they didn't get what they were after, they would just phase her out.

She refused to believe that all men were only after one thing—but so far, she had very little proof to the contrary. None, actually.

Jorge laughed at her response, amused that she was so honest. He was used to women who liked to be mysterious, to exercise their feminine wiles on him. In reality, a great many of them were about as shallow as saucers—not that he required much depth in his partner of the moment. It made things far less complicated that way.

But this one was different.

This one didn't seem at all versed in the flirtatious give-and-take that went on between the male and female of the species. Rather than being as devious as a cat, she came across more like Bambi, with all of the famous fawn's innocence.

A trace of guilt began to nibble away at him. Jorge was beginning to regret his bet with Ricky. He hadn't counted on the fact that there might very well be feelings involved. And there were. He could see it in Jane's luminous eyes.

He also hadn't counted on the fact that he would be attracted to his target. Not just physically, but in a way that he couldn't even quite put into words.

Jorge certainly couldn't pin this feeling on alcohol consumption because he hadn't really consumed any. Just one quick toast of white wine with his parents, sisters and their spouses before the Fortune Foundation party had officially gotten under way. But since then, he hadn't had anything stronger to drink than a ginger ale.

No, Jorge couldn't blame his reaction to Jane on anything other than the petite woman herself.

He wasn't sure how he felt about that, so, for the time being, he decided not to think about it.

"You're laughing at me," Jane protested self-consciously, the aura of her out-of-body experience beginning to fade just a little.

The faint pink color he witnessed creeping up her rather seductive high cheekbones was oddly arousing, Jorge mused. With the rest of the evening stretching out before him, he decided he definitely wanted to get to know this woman better and discover what made her so different from the legions of other women he'd known—other than her obvious lack of sophistication and her innocent manner.

"I'm not laughing at you," Jorge told her gently. "I'm laughing with you."

Now even she knew that was a line. Or was he just poking fun at her? "You might not have noticed," she pointed out quietly, "but I'm not laughing."

Jorge didn't answer immediately. Instead, he slipped his hand behind her head, cupping it.

For a moment, she thought he was going to kiss her again and she could have sworn that the wattage at Red went down several notches as the very room grew dark. She struggled to hang on to her consciousness.

"Sure you are," Jorge told her. "I can see it in your eyes."

The very remark coaxed a smile to her lips, whether out of nervousness or just because being so near to this dynamic, gorgeous man made her want to smile all over, she really didn't know. For the moment, she didn't care, either. What mattered was the proximity. She wanted to remain this close to

Jorge for as long as humanly possible without having to resort to handcuffs.

God, she was babbling and her lips weren't even moving.

Things like this didn't happen to people like her, she thought again. And while it *was* happening, she was just going to go with it and enjoy it.

Because she knew it was never, ever going to happen again.

"If you say so," Jane answered, her voice deliberately low to keep it from cracking.

Did she have any idea how sexy she sounded, Jorge wondered.

He had a feeling that she didn't, that Jane Gilliam had probably gone through her whole life seriously underestimating herself. It didn't take a student of women to pick up on that. He could tell by her body language and by the very way she wore her clothes. She dressed nicely, but there was no sign that there had been any extra fussing, any extra care taken. The same applied to her makeup.

He caught himself wondering about her. Really wondering about her as a person, not a conquest.

Leaning his head against Jane's, he looked into her eyes, then he shifted so that his lips were near her ear. "Who are you, Jane Gilliam?" he asked her quietly.

His breath sent warm shivers up and down her spine, and she was afraid he'd see how very inexperienced she was—he'd probably already guessed that anyway.

Why had he kissed her, she wondered again. A man

like this wouldn't have been alone any night of the year, especially not one that was considered to be the most important. She curbed the urge to ask, sensing that the answer might send her plummeting to the ground.

Jane felt as if she were trapped inside some kind of bubble—and bubbles always burst. There was no getting away from that. But not just yet.

Not just now.

Jane ran the tip of her tongue along her bottom lip. What was he asking her?

"Do you mean what do I do for a living?"

"That's as good a start as any," he acknowledged, aware that any one of a number of women he knew would have taken the question and given him some sort of existential, philosophical answer. Jane, apparently, was grounded.

His mother, he realized, would love her.

Jorge quickly glanced around, hoping that Maria Mendoza wasn't standing somewhere close by, taking all this in. She'd misunderstand immediately, especially since Jane was not like any of the other women he kept company with.

"I work for Red Rock ReadingWorks," Jane told him, tripping over the alliteration for the first time since she'd joined the organization. If she wasn't careful, any second she was going to start sounding like a chatty fool. "That's a nonprofit organization that—"

Jorge held up his hand to stop her before she

launched into a lengthy description of Reading-Works and all the services that it offered.

"I'm familiar with ReadingWorks," he told her.

She clamped her jaw shut to keep it from dropping in surprise. "You are?" The next moment, Jane realized her oversight. "Of course you are. You said that Isabella was your cousin." And the pretty thirty-year-old dropped by the storefront building where Reading-Works was housed often enough. Isabella probably had mentioned the place to him once or twice.

Jane felt self-conscious. She always did when attention was focused on her. She made an attempt to deflect it back to him. Besides, she really did want to find out a few things about this man who had set her on fire.

"What do you do?"

He glanced at the glass on the table, the one he'd initially offered to fill. "Well, tonight, I'm a bartender."

She sincerely doubted that bartending was Jorge's sole occupation. He looked far too vital, far too intelligent to be satisfied with mixing drinks and wiping down a counter.

"And other nights?" she prompted. "And days?" Jane added quickly when she realized what her initially innocent question had to sound like to him.

Broad shoulders shrugged casually beneath his royal blue shirt. His easygoing grin nonetheless created a knot in the pit of her stomach.

"A little of this, a little of that." He saw the curiosity in her eyes. She really wanted to know, he thought. Most women just wanted to see the size of his billfold—among other things. "I'm an entrepreneur," he added.

"That sounds interesting. Tell me about it."

She actually sounded genuinely interested, he thought. Before he knew it, he began talking about his latest venture.

Oh man, what an operator Jorge was, Ricky Jamison thought, standing over in a corner and watching his idol's every move. Because he was so far away and there was so much noise, Ricky couldn't hear what was being said, but he could certainly see what was going on. Within the space of a few minutes—and, from the looks of it, one hell of a kiss—Jorge had brought the bookish woman to a melting point.

Ricky sighed, shaking his head. His friend Josh and Josh's girlfriend, Lindsey, had their heads together over in the corner, sharing something private. Ricky felt a pang as he wished he had that kind of ability, to make girls fall for him.

When he was older, Ricky thought wistfully, he wanted to be exactly like Jorge Mendoza. The man was a god in his eyes.

Patrick Fortune rang in this New Year's the very same way he rang in all the others since he'd met his bride: by kissing Lacey.

His arm rested comfortably around his still-beautiful wife's shoulders as he surveyed the very crowded banquet hall. He recognized almost all the faces here, and that was his own doing—his and Maria Mendoza's. It wasn't every New Year's Eve that he managed to gather together so many members of his family under one roof. Sadly, not all of his five children and their spouses could make it. But on the bright side, his brother William and William's five children were all here, as well as Cynthia's children.

Bolder than sunlight, Cynthia had always marched to a different drummer and made her own rules, usually as she went along. Still, he wished she'd taken him up on the invitation and come. He wanted *all* his siblings here, all his nieces and nephews as well as his own children. Not because he had any special announcement to make, but just because he felt the need for their presence.

Family was everything.

The older he became, the more inclined Patrick felt to forget any past grievances that might have once caused him to turn his back on one member of the family or another. Life was too short—and it was getting shorter all the time. He'd thought that his cousin Ryan would live forever and Ryan had been dead now for four years. It seemed impossible, and yet it was true.

He still missed the man a great deal.

The swish of Lacey's dress as she turned toward him caught his attention.

"A penny for your thoughts," she said, leaning in so that he could hear her. He'd looked entirely too pensive for the last few minutes and she wondered if there was anything wrong.

Patrick laughed at the way she'd asked her question. "And that," he declared, his mouth curving in amusement, "is how our fortune continues to remain intact. Your frugality."

"Very funny." She threaded her arm through his as she looked up at him. He was still an exceptionally handsome man, she caught herself thinking. "Where are you right now?"

Patrick patted her arm. "Right here beside you, my love." He sighed. "Just missing Ryan, that's all. He used to love family gatherings like this."

Ryan Fortune had been a good man who always saw the best in people. Lacey liked to think that Patrick was the same way. She tightened her hold on his arm. "He wouldn't want you to be sad, Patrick."

Lacey was right. As always. He supposed that what had triggered his thoughts was seeing Lily tonight—Ryan's widow. Seeing her made him expect to see Ryan somewhere in her immediate vicinity. If only.

"No, you're right, he wouldn't. Just give me a minute to get my party face back in place," he teased.

Just then, someone bumped into him, hard. If there had been any more space between him and Lacey, he might have actually fallen into her, bringing her down with him. Patrick turned to look at the man who had stumbled into him.

"Sorry," the other man apologized. "I think I've

had just a little too much to drink. I'm going to get some air," he said by way of an excuse.

"Good idea," Patrick agreed, addressing the words to the back of the man's head. He stared after him for a second. There was something vaguely familiar about the man, but most likely, it could have just been his imagination. He shrugged his shoulders and returned to the party.

* * *

The man kept going, weaving his way in and out of the crowd, working his way to the front door. Once he was confident he was out of Patrick's sight, his meandering gait ceased.

One down, he thought, a self-satisfied smirk playing along his thin lips.

Chapter Four

Jane still couldn't quite believe how this evening had turned out. If it wasn't such a cliché, she would have actually pinched herself to see if she was dreaming.

Jorge had not left her side since he came to ask her about refilling her drink and then remained to utterly rock her world.

She finally understood what that phrase meant. This had to be what Californians experienced when a 7.5 earthquake hit. Even though it was after one o'clock and the kiss that had all but turned her brain to mush, was an hour in the past, the ground beneath her feet still felt as if it were moving. Her insides were still in a state of flux.

But Jorge hadn't moved on.

After he'd kissed her, all but burning off her lips, he'd stayed with her. Talked with her.

And made her feel beautiful.

Even when the man behind the bar had finally managed to get his attention and signaled to him in an obvious entreaty to return to his post, rather than seizing the excuse and leaving her, Jorge had laced his fingers through hers and had taken her along with him when he went to talk to the bartender.

"Hey, man, I need you to take over now," Angel said to him, stripping off the black half apron he'd donned earlier.

Jorge made no effort to take the apron from him. Instead, he said, "Ask Carlos to take over," mentioning the name of one of the waiters working this evening. "He owes me a favor."

Angel sighed, stashing the apron beneath the bar for the time being. "If you say so."

Jane felt a little guilty, taking Jorge away from the job he was supposed to be helping out with. "I'm keeping you."

Jorge turned toward her and smiled into her eyes, creating yet another huge tidal wave inside her stomach. "If that's what you want," he murmured.

Jane forgot to breathe again.

When she remembered, after a beat, she tried to draw it in subtly and then release it slowly. She was sure he'd noticed.

God, but she was acting as sophisticated as an escapee from a fifteenth-century nunnery. She really was going to have to get a grip on herself.

But Jorge was like no other man she'd ever met.

He was still holding her hand and that, somehow, was impeding the flow of blood to her brain. She had to concentrate in order to think.

"No, I meant..." She searched for the right words. "That I'm taking you away from your work."

"Not my work," he corrected her. "I'm just helping out, remember?"

Right, she thought, he'd already said something about that, about being a businessman, an entrepreneur, not a bartender. Damn, her head felt like a sieve, with all the information she was receiving just leaking out of every pore. She wasn't like this normally. Ordinarily, she absorbed details like a sponge and retained absolutely everything.

Not this time.

"And for the most part," Jorge was saying, his low, sexy voice working its way under her skin, thrilling her, "the party's beginning to wind down."

Even as he said it, a wave of cold air wove through the room as the front doors opened and several people made their way out into the night. It was mild as far as winters around here went, but there was no denying that it was still cold.

More than anything, Jane didn't want the evening to end. But even Cinderella had to go home at midnight, and she'd already beaten Cinderella's record by an hour.

Without thinking, Jane ran the tip of her tongue along her lips. She could still taste him. If she closed her eyes, she could still feel the pressure of his lips against hers.

This was definitely one New Year's Eve she was going to remember for the rest of her life—no matter how long she lived.

As if sensing what she was thinking, Jorge asked, "Can I take you home, Jane? Or did you drive over here by yourself?"

Why did that sound as if she was such a loser, coming to a New Year's Eve party by herself? Besides, she hadn't come alone, she'd come here with Isabella.

But it had been a long time since she'd seen her friend. Scanning the immediate area now, she couldn't find Isabella.

"I came with Isabella," Jane told him, still searching through the sea of faces for a glimpse of her friend.

The answer coaxed out another smile. "Isabella won't mind if I bring you home," he assured her.

Jane stopped searching and looked at him. "But how will she know? Isabella might get worried if she can't find me."

Now that was downright refreshing, Jorge thought, impressed. He'd hooked up with any number of women at parties who'd left girlfriends—and boyfriends—wandering around looking for them without so much as a second thought. Their focus was exclusively on their own pleasure.

Jane Gilliam was certainly different from the type of woman he was accustomed to. Maybe she deserved closer scrutiny, he mused. Her kiss had been a definite surprise. Maybe there were other surprises to be uncovered as well.

"Don't worry," he told her, "I'll leave word at the hostess desk for her. She's bound to ask there if she can't find you."

Jane hesitated—but not too much. She *really* wanted to be with Jorge for as long as possible.

"Well, if you think it's all right."

She couldn't keep from smiling. Everything inside her was cheering. The evening wasn't ending yet. She'd gotten a reprieve. Who knew, once they got to her apartment, maybe he'd stay a while for coffee and conversation. She loved listening to the sound of his voice.

Amused by her shy eagerness, Jorge ran the back of his knuckles along her cheek, then watched, fascinated, as a small nerve along her cheekbone winked in and out as if it was flirting with him.

"I think it's all right," he assured her.

From across the room, Maria Mendoza was in the middle of instructing several of the busboys to subtly begin gathering up dishes that had clearly been abandoned when she suddenly noticed her son talking to a young woman. Not just talking to her, but leaning in the way he did when he'd singled someone out.

Squinting, Maria looked closer. For once, the woman who had caught her son's attention didn't look as if she was modeling all the makeup offered at a department display counter. In fact, she looked almost sweet. There was nothing brash or flashy about her. And the dress she was wearing wasn't cut down to her navel.

She was the kind of young woman, Maria thought as she abruptly stopped addressing the busboys, that she would have personally hand-selected for Jorge.

She knew her, she realized. Jane…something. Jane Gilliam, that was it. She'd met her once through Patrick Fortune. He spoke very highly of the young woman's selflessness and her dedication to the children she worked with, as well as her passionate pledge to help every child to learn how to read.

Several times during the evening, she'd noted that the poor girl was sitting off by herself. At one point, Jane had even taken out a book from her purse and had begun to read. While everyone else had been enjoying themselves, the shy young woman clearly felt cut off by loneliness.

Well, she obviously wasn't lonely anymore, Maria thought, pleased. Not with Jorge talking to her. Jane seemed to be hanging on his every word.

Maria's mother's heart swelled with hope and joy. Could Jorge finally, *finally* be growing up? Could he finally be abandoning that wanton side that had him going from one shallow beauty to another? Had he left that life behind him to turn his attention to a woman of substance?

She fervently hoped so. Maybe all those prayers to St. Jude, patron saint of hopeless causes, were finally paying off.

"Señora Mendoza?" Luis, one of the busboys

hesitantly tried to get her attention. "You did not finish telling us what you wanted us to do."

She needed to get over there, Maria thought, to find out if what she was seeing was real. "Do what you are paid to do, Luis," Maria told the young man. He needed to show a little initiative if he ever hoped to be anything more than just a busboy. "Must I do all the thinking for you?"

Luis looked a little chagrinned as he bowed his head. "No, Señora."

Maria patted his arm. "Good, then get to it, please."

Even as she spoke, she quickly began making her way through the revelers who were still left. But her eyes never left her target: Jorge and the young woman. Though no longer in her thirties, Maria prided herself on still being very quick on her feet when she wanted to be.

She made it to her son's side before he had a chance to get away.

Placing a hand on his shoulder, she could see that she'd caught him by surprise. Good. "Are you leaving, Jorge?" she asked innocently.

"Yes, in a few minutes, Mama." And then, for form's sake—and because he loved her—he added, "If you don't mind."

"Of course I don't mind," Maria assured him magnanimously even as her eyes covertly darted toward Jane and then back again. "You've been a great help tonight. Your father is very grateful. There were more people here than were expected."

Maria paused, waiting. But Jorge was not taking

the hint. He wasn't making any introductions. Maria was not shy about taking matters into her own hands. It was how she'd gotten to where she was now.

She turned toward Jane, a bright smile on her face. "Hello, you might not remember me, but we met—"

It was only around good-looking men that Jane found herself almost hopelessly tongue-tied, feeling about as sharp as a button. When dealing with the rest of the world, she became friendly and cheery, which was more her natural state.

She smiled warmly now at the older woman. "Of course I remember you, Señora Mendoza. Mr. Fortune introduced us last year. He speaks very highly of you every time your name comes up."

She was gracious as well as sweet, Maria thought. "As he does you," Maria responded.

For a moment, Jorge almost felt as if he were on the outside looking in. It wasn't a situation he was accustomed to. Moreover, his mother's behavior was a bit of a surprise. She wasn't usually this friendly with any of the women he charmed.

Bemused, Jorge looked from Jane to his mother. He could read his mother's mind as clearly as if the words had been written on a huge billboard and hung around her neck.

Sorry, Ma, not going to happen, he thought.

Granted, Jane was special in her own unique way and he had to admit that he was attracted and somewhat captivated by her, but neither condition meant that he was about to suddenly abandon his bachelor life for this woman with the huge, soulful brown eyes. At most, he'd get further acquainted with her, spend a little time pleasuring them both, and then move on. It was his way.

"I was just about to take Jane home," he told his mother. "She came with Isabella, so if you see her, just let her know that I've taken care of Jane's transportation for the evening."

"Of course." Maria's smile was just a tad strained as she offered it to Jane. Turning, Maria began to leave but at the last moment, she buttonholed her son and whispered a warning into his ear. "Don't you hurt this one." Releasing him, she smiled broadly. This time, there was nothing forced about it. Before leaving for good, she looked over her shoulder at Jane and said, "I hope I will see you again very soon."

Me, too, Señora. Me, too, Jane couldn't help thinking, even though she knew the chances of that happening were very, very slim.

Jorge waited until his mother disappeared into the crowd. The woman really did have eyes in the back of her head, he thought. Turning to Jane, he inclined his head and asked, "Ready?"

He wouldn't believe just how ready she was, Jane thought. "I just have to get my coat," she told him. She pointed vaguely in the general direction of the coatroom.

There was a crowd around the desk, Jorge noted. No sense in their both standing around, waiting their turn. He'd have better luck getting to the front of the line if he went alone.

"Why don't you give me the claim number?" Jorge suggested. "I'll go get it for you."

She wasn't accustomed to such attentive gallantry. Usually, she was the one running the errands. Flipping open the clip on her clutch purse, she began searching through it.

"It's here someplace," Jane murmured. She was forced to go through the purse twice before she finally located the small, square card with the red claim number on it. "Here it is," she announced triumphantly.

Jorge took the claim number from her, his fingers lightly, deliberately brushing against hers. He could see by the look in her eyes that he'd succeeded in sending yet another shock wave dancing through her body. Her reaction amused him and yet, there was something almost touchingly sweet about it.

It was enough to make him feel guilty—if he wasn't enjoying himself so much.

"I'll be right back," he promised. "Don't go anywhere."

There wasn't a chance of that, she thought. Not even if they used dynamite. "I won't," she promised.

Jane watched as he walked away, utterly mesmerized by the rhythmic movement of his hips. Utterly mesmerized by everything about him.

Jorge really seemed to like her, she thought, stunned and awed and very thrilled. She had no idea why someone like him would have even stopped to give her the time of day, but right now, she didn't want to dig too deeply. Didn't want to risk the chance of all this suddenly fading away. For now, she was going to ride this wonderful wave for as long as she possibly could.

Sighing, she closed her eyes and smiled to herself. Maybe, just this once, nice girls didn't have to finish last.

"Didn't I tell you he was terrific?"

Jane picked out the young voice from amid a sea of others and opened her eyes again. For a second, she thought whoever was speaking was talking to her. But as she turned around to look, she saw that the owner of the voice, a young teenager who looked about fourteen, maybe fifteen, but just barely, was talking to another, slightly older looking youth.

She turned back around, not wanting the boys to think that she was eavesdropping on their conversation.

But it was hard not to. The younger of the two sounded so enthusiastic.

"All I had to do was point someone out and he had her eating out of his hand in less than five minutes," he marveled. "He said it was easy, that all it took was just a matter of making the girl think she was the prettiest one in the room, the center of his attention. But it's gotta be more than that," Ricky insisted.

"Well, du-uh," Josh responded condescendingly. "When you look like Jorge Mendoza, all you have to do is stand still and half a dozen drooling women come running to you. It doesn't exactly take an Einstein to figure that out, Ricky."

"I don't know," Ricky countered. "I mean, he's a

great-looking guy and all, but this woman I picked out, she looked a little standoffish. I really didn't think Jorge could melt her as fast as he did." He shook his head in quiet admiration. "But five minutes after he came up to her, he was kissing her." He paused to laugh softly. "*Really* ringing in the New Year, if you know what I mean."

The one called Ricky was grinning broadly. She could hear it in his voice, even as Jane's heart froze in her chest.

"I think he's taking her to his place," she heard the young teenager speculate to his friend. "That wasn't part of the bet, but—"

"You actually bet him, you idiot?" the other teen asked incredulously.

Ricky bristled. "Not money," he protested. "It's just that I didn't think he could do it *that* fast. I just said the word. Like 'I bet you can't.'"

She heard the other boy scoff. "I could have told you that you'd lose."

Jane felt sick. For a second, she was afraid she might throw up.

They were talking about *her*.

That was why Jorge had approached her out of the blue—because he'd made a bet with a teenager who wasn't even old enough to shave yet.

How stupid of her to think that a guy like Jorge Mendoza would be attracted to her. To think that he might have even liked her a tiny bit.

A bet.

Jane could feel angry tears forming in her eyes.

She couldn't remember ever, *ever* feeling this humiliated. This awful.

She couldn't stay here, couldn't wait for him to come back. She never wanted to see that honey-tongued bastard again. Who did he think he was, making her the object of a bet? she thought angrily.

Clutching her purse to her chest, Jane swung around and forged a path to the front door. She bumped into people as she went, murmuring half-hearted excuses as she passed them.

It was cold outside. Remnants of snow from the last storm crunched beneath her high heels, but she didn't care.

Wrapping her arms around herself, she searched for a passing taxi to flag down.

There were none out on the street this time of night. Why? Didn't they know it was New Year's Eve?

Shivering, she hurried down several blocks and then took shelter in the doorway of an office building. She placed a call to a taxi service on her cell phone and waited for her ride.

And cried angry tears.

Chapter Five

"Patrick, if you want me to take that suit to the cleaners tomorrow, please don't forget to empty out your pockets," Lacey told her husband the next morning as she popped her head into the master bedroom.

The bright morning sun was trying to push its way into the room despite the heavy drapes at the windows that barred its passage. It was one of the rare mornings that Patrick actually slept in.

Sitting up now, Patrick ran his hand through his tousled reddish hair. Despite the odd hint of white, he still looked boyish, especially with sleep still hovering around his eyes.

He reached for his glasses on the nightstand and

put them on. The world came into focus, as did the digital clock next to the lamp.

He always thought of himself as energetic—except when compared to his wife. "Lacey, it's New Year's Day. It's a holiday. What are you doing up so early and why are we talking about dry cleaning?"

She crossed to him and stood before the bed that she had vacated more than an hour before.

"I'm up, dear husband, because, in case you've forgotten, we're having some of the family over for a late lunch today, and I'm talking about dry cleaning because someone," she looked at him pointedly, "spilled coffee on his jacket last night." She ran her hand along his stubbled face affectionately. "And just because it's a technical holiday doesn't mean that the world suddenly stops spinning."

"Technical?" he echoed, just a little perplexed at her meaning.

"Technical," she repeated. "Do you have any idea how many sales are going on at this very moment as you are lounging around in your PJs?"

Getting out of bed, Patrick groaned. "I could never understand that. Why would anyone want to get up that early just to go shopping? What kind of bargains could they possibly offer to warrant that?"

Sometimes the man she loved could be adorably naive, Lacey thought. She laughed at the look on his face, then stopped to pick up the shirt he must have dropped on the floor last night—or early this morning. He'd been pretty tired as she recalled.

"Spoken like a man who has never had to search for a bargain in his life."

"My biggest bargain," Patrick freely confessed as he came up behind her and enfolded his wife in an affectionate embrace, "was finding you and making you my wife. Anything that happened after that would only be deemed anticlimatic."

"You do know how to turn a lady's head," she told him with a warm smile. "But I'm not going to be distracted." Draping his shirt over her arm, she looked around for the suit she'd mentioned. "Where are the rest of your clothes from the party?"

He released her. "The cleaners aren't having a sale, are they?" he asked, amused.

"I just want to put the suit aside while I think of it," she told him. One finely shaped eyebrow arched over a sparkling green eye. "Remember leaving your house key in your pants pocket the last time? Remember wasting all that time, looking for it?"

Patrick inclined his head. "Point well taken," he allowed with a sigh.

He moved to his side of the walk-in closet. He'd meant to hang the suit back up, but somehow, it had only made it to the floor of the closet. Picking up the pants and jacket, he quickly checked all four pants pockets.

"Empty," he announced, handing the slightly wrinkled gray slacks to Lacey.

"And the jacket?" she asked as she dropped the pants on top of the shirt she had over her arm.

He checked the right pocket. He distinctly remembered taking out his wallet and depositing his keys beside it on the bureau. But as he slipped his fingers into the left outer pocket, he frowned. His fingers had come in contact with something.

It was a folded piece of paper and he opened it up as he removed the paper from his pocket. He had no memory of putting it in his pocket, no memory of anyone handing it to him.

He scanned the small sheet quickly, his frown deepening slightly.

"Not so empty, is it?" Lacey teased, then saw his expression. Something was clearly wrong, Lacey thought. "What's the matter?"

Not waiting for him to answer, she came closer in order to read the note, which was printed in large block letters.

"ONE OF THE FORTUNES IS NOT WHO YOU THINK."

It was Lacey's turn to be puzzled. She looked up at her husband for enlightenment. "Who gave this to you?"

He turned it over in his hand. There was nothing on the back. "I have no idea."

A touch of apprehension wove through her. "A note just turns up in your pocket and you have no idea where it came from?"

Rather than crumple it and toss it into the waste-paper basket, he placed it on the bureau. This required closer scrutiny. But not when Lacey was around. He didn't want to alarm her.

"That about sums it up," he agreed.

It was Lacey's turn to frown as anticipation got the better of her. "Do you think that it's some kind of warning?"

"I think it's some kind of waste of paper." Patrick handed her the jacket. "Here you go, one suit, as per your request." And then he gave her a quick, courtly bow. "Now, if milady doesn't mind, I'd really like to take a shower."

She nodded, the note already relegated to a thing of the past unless something more about it came up. Right now, she had a lunch to oversee.

"When you're done with your shower," she told him, "I've got a few things I need you to do."

He grinned and kissed her quickly. He'd expected nothing less.

"Of course you do."

But as soon as Lacey was gone, Patrick picked up the telephone next to the bed and called his brother, William.

Younger by a year, William had an offbeat sense of humor. This might have been his idea of a joke, although, truthfully, Patrick did have his doubts that William's humor was *this* offbeat.

"Bill," he began when his brother picked up on the other end. "It's Patrick. Happy New Year," he prefaced, getting the amenities out of the way, even though he'd just seen his younger brother less than nine hours ago at the party.

"Same to you," William responded. "You know, this is rather a coincidence, you calling like this. I was just debating calling you."

There was an unsettling note in William's voice that caught his attention. "Oh?"

"Yeah."

William paused, hunting for the right words. He'd found himself later in life than Patrick had, finally making a niche for himself with Fortune Forecasting, a company that predicted stock market trends. But ever since his wife had died last year, he'd lost his focus again and had felt adrift. He'd begun to look toward Patrick for guidance again.

"Now this is going to sound a little off the wall," he finally said, "but I just found this note in my pocket this morning. It says—"

"—One of the Fortunes is not who you think," Patrick completed.

For a second there was stunned silence on the other end of the line. And then William laughed nervously. "So it was you."

He'd obviously missed something, Patrick thought. "Excuse me?"

"It was you," William repeated. "You were the one who put the note in my pocket," he elaborated when Patrick made no response. "I've got to say, this isn't your usual style, Patrick. What's the point?" he wanted to know.

"I have no idea what the point is," Patrick said, sitting down on the bed. "I didn't put the note in your pocket, William. As a matter of fact, I found an identical note in mine. Someone slipped it into my jacket." He tried to think of when that could have happened. The restaurant was fairly crowded all night. He'd been jostled any number of times during the evening.

He heard William sigh. "Well, that makes three, then."

"Three?" Patrick repeated, not sure where William was going with this.

"Three," William said again. "I just got off the phone with Lily," he said, referring to their late cousin Ryan's wife. "She just called. Someone slipped a note into her purse. She had no idea what to make of it. I told her I thought it was someone's inebriated idea of a joke."

Patrick looked at the note in his hand. "That was my first thought, too."

"And now?"

"And now I don't know," he admitted truthfully.

He was getting a very uneasy feeling about all this. Why would someone target all three of them with this note? And were they intended as warnings—or threats?

"What do you want to do about this?" William asked.

"We sit tight until something else happens."

William sounded clearly disturbed. "Who do you think the note's referring to?"

As far as that went, Patrick hadn't a clue. "It still might be a joke, albeit a poor one."

"Nobody comes to mind?" William pressed.

There had been no long-lost second cousin, twice removed on the scene, no reason to believe that members of the family weren't who they were supposed to be.

"No one," he assured his brother. "Listen, I know you're coming over for lunch this afternoon. Bring the note with you. And tell Lily to do the same."

"What do you have in mind?"

"Nothing yet," Patrick said truthfully. "But it certainly wouldn't hurt to circle the wagons, just in case."

There was silence on the other end of the line and for a moment, Patrick thought William might offer an opinion or solution of his own. But when he finally spoke, it was just tacit agreement on his part. "I'll pass the word along to Lily."

"Thanks. I'll see you all later," Patrick said just before he hung up the receiver.

He was fairly certain he'd managed not to sound as concerned as he felt. It could very well be nothing, just some fool yanking their collective chains. But he was a Fortune and, contrary to the name, he and his family had had their share of adverse dealings.

It never hurt to be prepared.

Jorge stood in the center of the still-crowded restaurant, looking around. He felt exactly like the Prince must have just after Cinderella fled from him at the stroke of midnight.

Except that he was holding a light gray coat instead of a glass slipper. When he'd returned from the coatroom, she wasn't standing where he'd left her. She wasn't anywhere at all.

He spent the next twenty minutes scanning the room and describing her to people, asking them if they'd seen her. Finally, when he talked to the bartender who'd ultimately taken over for him, Carlos said he'd thought he'd seen her pushing her way to the front door. And yes, the man added, she wasn't wearing a coat, which had made him think it was rather odd.

Why, Jorge wondered. Why had she suddenly taken off like that? What would have made her leave without saying anything to him?

And without her coat? It didn't make any sense to him.

Everything about the woman aroused his interest.

Frustration ate away at him. He had no phone number for her, and no address either. He told himself to just go home and forget about it. But he couldn't.

Draping her coat on one arm, he took out his cell phone and dialed Information. With one hand pressed against his ear to drown out the surrounding noise, he gave the operator Jane's name and waited for a response.

She was unlisted.

It figured, he thought. Biting back a curse, Jorge stared at the coat he was holding.

What had made Jane bolt out of here like that? She'd given every indication that she liked being with him. So then what—?

"Did one get away from you?"

The question, spoken so close to him, nearly made him jump. Gloria was standing right behind him. Her husband Jack was next to her.

Jorge saw her looking at the coat, an amused expression on her face. Not what he needed right now, he thought. Squaring his shoulders, Jorge shifted the coat to his other arm. He'd already made up his mind that he was going to find Jane Gilliam and give her back her coat—and ask for an explanation—no matter what it took.

"Not for long," he told Gloria, his voice cocky. And then, just for a moment, he dropped his guard. "Did you see the woman I was with earlier?"

"The one Mama liked so much?" Gloria countered innocently. Maria had brought all three of her daughters' attention to Jorge and the woman he was talking to. "Yes, I did," Gloria added quickly before he could profess any denials. "She didn't look like your usual arm candy." Gloria patted his face affectionately. "Looks like you're finally growing up a little, big brother."

If she was baiting him, he wasn't about to bite, Jorge thought. He had more important things on his mind. "You didn't happen to see where she went, did you?"

Gloria shook her head, surprised. A woman avoiding Jorge? This had to be a first. "Sorry."

"Maybe someone told her about your reputation and it scared her off," Jack speculated as he helped Gloria on with her coat.

Gloria felt a tug on her heart, empathizing with her brother. She was certain this had to be the first time he'd ever experienced rejection on any level.

"If it helps any, I think I heard Jack's father say she works for Red Rock ReadingWorks. I could ask Mama to make sure—"

The second Gloria mentioned the organization, Jorge remembered Jane mentioning the name.

"ReadingWorks," he repeated. "That's right." Grateful, he kissed his sister's cheek. "Thanks."

Something different was going on here, Gloria thought, looking at her brother more closely. She'd never seen him like this about a girl. But then, as far as she knew, no girl had *ever* pulled a disappearing act on Jorge. If anything, it was always the other way around.

"Any time," Gloria murmured. She'd teased him about finally growing up, but maybe, just maybe, there was something to it.

If so, she thought, Mama was going to be thrilled.

January 2 was a typical cold winter day.

Jane shivered as she made her way to Reading-Works' front door. She was going to have to dip into her savings and buy another coat, she thought glumly. Wearing three sweaters, one on top of another, just didn't do the trick.

Maybe her coat was still at the restaurant, she thought hopefully. She'd call over there during her first break and inquire.

And pray that she didn't run into Jorge Mendoza.

Pushing open the front door, the warm air that met her was lovingly welcomed. At the same time, goose bumps formed all over her body.

Like the ones she'd felt when Jorge had kissed her New Year's Eve.

What in heaven's name could she have been thinking? Men like that didn't give women like her the time of day—unless, of course, there was a bet involved, she thought sarcastically.

Served her right for being so naive.

With a sigh, she shook her head. Well, it was a new year and it was back to reality for her. Time to put impossibly foolish dreams behind her.

Walking into the lounge where all the teachers gathered for their breaks and lunch, she saw that a number of her coworkers were clustered around the main table. At first, she thought that someone had brought in cookies. But then she saw that what had captured their attention was a huge profusion of flowers, nestled in a large basket that was in the center of the table.

Someone had gotten flowers, she thought with a touch of envy. She had no idea what that felt like, to have someone care enough about you to send flowers and publicly acknowledge his attachment to you.

"Who's the lucky girl?" she asked, trying to sound cheerful as she joined the group.

Sally Hillman turned to look at her, a huge grin on her lips. "You are."

Jane stared at her, positive she'd heard wrong. "What?"

"Joyce couldn't help herself," Harriet Ryan, another tutor, volunteered. Embarrassed, Joyce, the general secretary, made a strange, disparaging noise. "She read the card. Why didn't you tell us you knew Jorge Mendoza?" she wanted to know.

"When did you meet him?" another woman asked.

"Where?"

"Details, girl, give us details," Sally begged. "The rest of us are dying to know."

The questions all melded together into one cacophony of voices and noises as Jane leaned over the table and plucked the card from the basket. She felt as if she were moving in slow motion.

"New Year's Eve ended much too soon," the card said. "With affection, Jorge."

"With affection," Joyce echoed, looking over her shoulder at the card she'd already read. A huge sigh followed. "You've been holding out on us," she accused Jane.

"Yeah," Harriet chimed in. "Not very nice of you, Jane. Give."

And five sets of eyes turned their eager faces toward her.

Chapter Six

Unlike her former beauty queen mother—or maybe because of her—Jane had never liked being the center of attention. It made her uncomfortable.

"There's nothing to 'give,'" Jane told Harriet.

The women exchanged exasperated looks with one another, as if they thought she was holding out on them.

"Oh, come on, Jane," Cecilia Evans, the oldest of the group, pressed. "A man doesn't send flowers and sign his name 'with affection' if something isn't going on. Especially not a hunk like Jorge Mendoza."

Cecilia drove the point home. "*How* does he know you work here?"

Jane looked back at the flowers. They would have had her floating on air—if she didn't know what she knew. She almost wished she hadn't overheard those boys gossiping.

Most likely, Jorge had sent the flowers because he'd had qualms of conscience.

But then, she backtracked, why should he if he didn't know that she knew?

This was all getting very complicated. All she wanted to do was get to work, do what she did best, and forget about everything else.

Some people were meant to have romance in their lives and some weren't. She belonged to the "weren't" group and she was just going to have to learn how to deal with that and accept it.

More than anything, Jane didn't want to talk about Jorge or the flowers or anything that had to do with why they might have been sent. But she had never learned how to be rude or cut people off. She'd certainly never learned how to tell them to butt out.

So she lifted her shoulders in a vague shrug and admitted, "I told him where I work."

"When?" Joyce demanded excitedly. "When did you tell him?" The slender blonde shook her head when information didn't immediately come spilling out of Jane's mouth. "If I'd met Jorge Mendoza, every single last detail would have been up on my blog three minutes after I got home. Maybe two."

"I don't blog," Jane said, seizing on the stray item.

"You don't talk much, either," Cecilia grumbled. Two of the other women chimed in their agreement.

Jane pressed her lips together, suppressing a sigh. It wasn't her intention to seem secretive about the matter. It was just that she knew that these flowers, didn't really mean anything and honest though she was, she certainly wasn't about to tell her friends that Jorge had kissed her on a bet.

Some things you just didn't talk about. To *anyone*.

Looking at the circle of eager faces surrounding her, she decided to give them just the bare bones and hope they'd be satisfied with that.

"I met him at the New Year's Eve party I went to at Red, the one Emmett Jamison and his wife threw for the Fortune Foundation. I went representing ReadingWorks," she added quickly, in case any of them thought she had a special in with the elite circle of people the Fortunes usually associated with. As the one who had worked at ReadingWorks the longest, she'd been the logical one to invite. "I was afraid if I didn't go, it might insult Mr. Jamison."

They all knew that the Foundation had given ReadingWorks sizable grants in the last couple of years, and it was largely because of the Foundation that ReadingWorks' doors were opened to the children whose parents could not afford to pay for private tutoring.

"Right," Harriet said, waving her hand at Jane's explanation. "Get to the good part," she urged. "How did you meet Jorge?"

"Is he as good looking as his pictures?" Sally asked.

Jane had to be honest. She always was. There

were times when she considered it almost a congenital defect. "Better."

"So? Get on with it," Sally begged. "There had to be a lot of people there."

"There were." It had been so crowded and so noisy that she had trouble concentrating on her book when she'd taken it out.

"So how did you two meet?" Cecilia wanted to know. "Don't skip anything," she ordered before Jane could say answer.

"He asked me if I wanted to freshen up my drink—he was tending bar for his parents," Jane explained.

She knew she was being disjointed, that the facts were tumbling out like grains of rice from a hole in the bottom of the box, but it was hard for her to collect her thoughts under all this scrutiny. Especially since she was still having trouble reconciling herself to the fact that the single greatest experience of her young life was tied to a bet, making her—in her mind, at least—the butt of a cruel joke.

The fact that Jorge had sent a note like that with flowers just served to confuse and complicate everything that much more.

"And then?" Sally urged when Jane didn't elaborate. "This is like pulling teeth," she complained. "What did you do to get him to send you flowers?"

"I didn't do anything," Jane protested. *Except run away.*

Maybe that was it, she thought. Maybe he *was*

feeling guilty because she'd bolted and he suspected
that she knew about the bet.

Joyce frowned. This obviously wasn't making
any sense to her, or the others. "So that was it? He
asked you if you wanted your drink freshened and
then he just disappeared?"

"Well, no." Jane thought about the way he'd
looked at her and a smile curved her mouth involun-
tarily. "We talked a little. And then it was midnight
and—"

The mere memory made her body tingle.

Joyce's eyes widened. "He kissed you?"

Jane nodded her head. For a split second, a wave
of heat washed over her as, despite her best efforts
to block it, the memory replayed itself in her head.

"Yes."

"And? What was it like?" Sally demanded.

Jane had never mastered the art of nonchalance.
Besides, there had been nothing nonchalant about
the way Jorge kissed. He had literally made the earth
move beneath her feet. No matter what his motives
were, she had to give him his due in that department.

"Pretty terrific."

"And you're seeing him again," Sally assumed
eagerly, skimming her fingertip down along a plump,
pink rose petal.

Despite everything, a sliver of sadness skewered
through Jane as she answered. "No."

The other women looked at each other.

"But he sent flowers," Harriet insisted. "How can
you not see someone who sent you flowers?"

Because he doesn't want to see me. He just doesn't want to feel bad.

Jane kept the words to herself, searching for some kind of plausible answer that would make the others back off and leave her alone. This was hard enough to deal with without pretending that she was starry-eyed and walking on air.

Just then, April, the administrative assistant, came into the lounge. Excitement pulsated from every pore as she announced, "Jane, there's someone here to see you."

Thank God, Jane thought. She didn't care who it was as long as it gave her an excuse to get away from this impromptu Spanish Inquisition before the thumbscrews came out.

Jane glanced at her watch, trying to remember her schedule for the day. It was a little early for her first student, Melinda Perez, to be coming in. She wasn't due for at least another hour. But that was all right.

"Bring Mrs. Perez and her daughter to the class-room," she told April.

April shook her head, her straight dark hair bobbing from side to side like black windshield wipers. "It's not Mrs. Perez."

That caught her off guard. Mothers usually brought their children, not fathers. Maybe Mrs. Perez wasn't feeling well.

"Okay, show Mr. Perez and his daughter to the classroom. Better yet," she decided, moving toward the doorway, "I'll do it."

April stayed where she was, a ninety-eight-pound

roadblock. She looked unsettled, Jane thought, and rather dazed, wearing what could only be termed a silly grin on her face.

"April, is something the matter?" Jane asked.

"It's not Mr. Perez either," the young girl said breathlessly.

Confused, Jane walked out into the hallway and saw why April was acting so flustered.

Jorge Mendoza stood just inside the doorway, with her winter coat draped over one arm and what looked like a picnic basket suspended from the other.

The grin on his lips was guaranteed to raise body temperatures by at least five degrees as far away as the next county.

"Hi, Jane. You forgot something at the restaurant the other night," he told her, his voice low and melodic as he held her coat slightly aloft.

By now, all of Jane's coworkers had poured out into the hallway. She could feel them standing behind her, a hyperventilating Greek chorus.

Just what she needed, an audience.

How much worse was this going to get? And why, knowing what she did, did her kneecaps feel as if they were dissolving right out from under her?

"Thank you," she murmured, accepting the coat he held out to her.

God, but he was even better looking in the light of day than he had been at the restaurant. But what was he doing here?

Maybe he'd made another bet, she said to herself.

Jorge drew a little closer to her, aware that they

were both under intense scrutiny. "Could I see you in private?"

Her uneasiness heightened. What was he up to? "I've got students coming in."

"Not for another hour," Jorge countered. He saw the surprise in her eyes and smiled. Nodding toward April, he said, "I checked."

"I can cover for you," Harriet volunteered. "I don't have anyone coming in until this afternoon."

"I can cover for you, too," Sally chimed in eagerly, her eyes never leaving Jorge.

His smile widening, Jorge gave a slight bow of his head. "Thank you, ladies. I promise I won't keep her too long."

Jane wanted to say something about the bet. Right here, right now, she wanted to give this too-handsome-for-his-own-good-or-anyone-else's a dressing down. Wanted to tell him that if he'd discovered a conscience and was here to make amends, she didn't want any part of that. She just wanted to be left alone.

She wanted to say all that. But the desire to get all of that off her chest was outweighed by the fact that she'd always hated making a scene. Jane absolutely despised displays of temper, maybe because she'd been the target of her mother's so often when she was growing up.

Whatever the reason, she swallowed her retort and kept it to herself, refusing to vent in front of her coworkers.

"All right, we can go to my classroom," she told him, resigned.

He laughed softly under his breath as he threaded his arm through hers. "First time I've ever looked forward to going to a classroom."

Several members of her Greek chorus giggled. Doing her best to ignore them—and the heat traveling up her body where Jorge was holding her—Jane led the way to the room where she did her tutoring. Jorge dropped his hand, allowing her to cross the threshold first.

Shutting the door behind her, Jane turned to look at him.

Charade over, she thought. *Time to dig up that backbone of yours, Janie.*

"Why did you come here?" she asked him.

He nodded toward the coat she was still holding. "I thought you might need your coat." He also wanted to know what had caused her to run off the other night, but for the moment, that could wait.

Jane had to admit that she was grateful to be reunited with her coat, but that still didn't explain the other thing he'd brought with him. "And you decided to pack it in a picnic basket?"

He set the basket down on the desk. "No, I packed some of my father's famous enchiladas and nachos in the basket, along with—" He rattled off several Mexican delicacies that he'd brought, ending with chocolate chip sweet bread.

The latter had always been her weakness and guilty pleasure. Had he known that?

No, of course not. How could he? Not even the people she worked with knew that about her. For the most part, she was a very private person. It had been a lucky guess on his part, nothing more.

"Why would you do that?" she wanted to know. She wasn't ordinarily suspicious, but after the other night, she'd decided that being cautious was a much wiser path for her to take.

Jorge opened the basket and took out a checkered tablecloth, which he proceeded to spread on the floor right behind her desk and chair. She watched him in surprised silence. Was he actually planning on pretending they were having a picnic?

"Because it might help make you forgive me," Jorge told her and then added an extremely soulful, "I'm sorry."

I'm sorry.

Her heart twisted in her chest. What was it about those words that could always make her forgive a myriad of transgressions and make her want everything to be right again? Was she just terminally kind-hearted—or a pushover?

Jane was tempted to say something about overhearing the two teens talking about the bet he'd made, but she hesitated too long and Jorge was talking again. Talking and burrowing his way into a heart that should have, by all rights, been hardened against him.

But wasn't.

"I don't know what would have made you run off like that, especially without your coat, but if it had to do with me," Jorge continued as he placed two plates and two sets of cutlery down on the tablecloth, "I really am sorry."

His wording made her realize that he had no idea that she'd overheard the two teens talking. And he probably had no remorse for making that kind of bet. This was a matter of ego. He was voicing a blanket apology because he just didn't like having a woman walk out on him.

She had to keep reminding herself of that, but being so close to him was having a definite effect on her thought process. As well as on her whole body.

What was the point of telling him that she'd overheard? That she knew she was nothing more than a bet to him? Saying it wouldn't change anything. So she looked away and said, "I had an emergency."

Two glasses joined the plates, cutlery and napkins. "What kind of an emergency?" he asked mildly.

She hadn't expected him to probe. Resorting to fabrications wasn't something that came easily to her, not even to save face. "The kind that made me hurry away," Jane responded vaguely.

Jorge looked at her for a long moment, then nodded. "Okay, you don't want to talk about it. I can respect that."

Too bad you can't respect me, Jane thought. But out loud, she said, "So, you see, you didn't have to go to all this trouble—"

"Well, since I did 'go to all this trouble,'" he said, echoing her words with a smile, "we might as well sit down and eat." Taking off his jacket, he folded it up into a square and then placed it on the floor in front of the place setting. He gestured for her to sit down on it. "Might be more comfortable that way," he explained.

She looked down at the food Jorge had placed on the tablecloth. It did look awfully good, she thought, especially since all she'd had today was half a Pop-Tart and yesterday, her appetite had deserted her completely and she'd hardly eaten at all.

"Okay," she agreed, sitting down on the jacket. She felt the material give beneath her. "I guess it wouldn't do any harm to eat."

"Nope, no harm at all." He got down on the floor, crossing his legs lotus-fashion. "You know, I like to think that I'm pretty good at reading people—"

About to start eating, she raised her eyes to his face. "Then maybe you're in the wrong place. We just read books here."

For as long as he could remember, women had come on to him. He'd never had a woman back away. But Jane Gilliam was definitely backing away, blocking all his best moves and his efforts at breaching her walls. Why? It wasn't ego, but curiosity and a certain fascination that spurred him on.

"Did I do something to upset you, Jane?" When she didn't answer, he took a guess. "Was it the flowers? Was sending them here embarrassing?"

She supposed that was as good an excuse to use as any. "It did put me on the hot seat."

Jorge laughed. Whenever he sent flowers to a woman, he always made sure there was maximum exposure involved, not because he was sending them but because he knew that women liked other women to see that they were the center of someone's attention. Jane was definitely different. And that really piqued his interest.

"You don't like all that attention, do you?" he guessed.

"No," she answered truthfully. "I don't."

"I have to admit, you are nothing like a lot of other women I've known." And right now, he thought, he had to admit that he was drawn to her because of that.

Jane had no doubt that he had known enough women to populate a small city. "I've always been a private person," she told him.

"A little mystery makes things interesting."

She hadn't meant it like that. Femme fatales were mysterious, not her. What you saw was what you got, she thought. But before she could say anything, Jorge was leaning forward.

Invading her space.

Making her pulse jump.

"Do you mind?" he asked.

The words left her lips in slow motion. "Mind what?" she asked in a hushed voice as he took her chin in his hand.

"You've got a little sauce right there." Moving his thumb slowly across the corner of her mouth, Jorge wiped the sauce away. "Got it."

He smiled at her just before he licked the side of his thumb.

Jane couldn't draw her eyes away. The sauce disappeared between his lips.

He'd done it again.

He'd made the air stand still in her lungs. If this kept up, her brain was going to malfunction because of a lack of oxygen.

If it hadn't already.

Chapter Seven

It took Jane a second to pull herself together and she had a feeling that he knew it. But there was no self-satisfied smirk on his face, no hint of a superior smile on his lips. If he did know what he was doing to her, he wasn't showing it.

She still had no idea why Jorge was here, sharing a picnic with her. Was this all part of his initial bet, or had it evolved into some elaborate plan to prove that he could get any woman he wanted with minimal effort? Was there some prize waiting for him at the goal line, depending on her reaction to him?

But even if it was that, why should she be his target? It wasn't as if she had some sort of reputation for being a removed, yet desirable ice princess. There was no one beating a path to her door. She was just an old-fashioned girl, someone her grandmother would have called a sweet bookworm—and her mother would have ridiculed.

If she held on to that thought, on to the knowledge that at best this was just some kind of a fleeting whim on Jorge's part—for whatever reason—then maybe she could keep a tighter rein on herself and not get carried away.

Or grow hopeful.

Just enjoy the moment, as you would if you were getting lost in a book, she ordered herself as she continued eating what, in all likelihood, was the best chicken enchilada she'd ever had. Books always ended and so would this. She had to remember that whatever was going on, however wonderful it might feel for the moment, it was all just fiction. Just like the books she loved to read.

Before she realized it, she'd finished eating. Picking up the napkin he'd put out, Jane wiped her fingers. "That was excellent," she told him.

"I'll pass that along to my father," he told her. "He'll be pleased." Jorge reached for the covered serving dish that he'd placed back in the basket. "There's more if you like."

"No, one was fine," she said quickly before he could place another enchilada on her plate. "I'll explode if I eat another one. Besides—" she smiled, nodding at the plate of stacked chocolate chip desserts "—I need to leave room for the sweet bread."

He liked the way her eyes seemed to light up when she smiled. "So you have a sweet tooth."

"Guilty as charged."

Jorge placed a sweet bread on a napkin and put it in front of her. "I'll remember that for next time."

"Next time?" she echoed.

Two small words, neither of which, by themselves, were unclear. But in this situation, combined and emerging from his mouth, she found herself unable to absorb them or figure out precisely what they meant—because Jorge couldn't possibly be saying what she thought he was saying. Wasn't this idyllic indoor picnic just a one-time thing?

"The next time we get together," Jorge elaborated and then suddenly stopped as a thought occurred to him. She'd been alone at the party, but that didn't necessarily mean that she was unattached. "Unless—are you seeing anyone?"

Not anymore, she thought. "No. I already told you I wasn't."

Her answer produced another smile on his lips. She stared at it, mesmerized. "Then it's all right if I see you again?"

If she didn't know better—and she did—she would have thought that Jorge was acting almost shy. But that was impossible. Jorge Mendoza had never had a shy day in his life. In a relatively small town like Red Rock, everyone knew everyone else, or at least *about* everyone else. And she knew about Jorge, knew that the impossibly handsome man went through women like tissues.

At thirty-eight, was it possible that Jorge had gone through every desirable woman in Red Rock and was now trolling for female companionship down at her level? Not that she thought of herself as beneath him, but the women he tended to pursue came from a more sophisticated social circle than she did. Their idea of charity meant writing a check while hers meant getting down in the trenches and becoming personally involved.

"If that's what you want," she heard herself answer. She watched his expression intently, waiting for him to shout, "April Fool's" even though they were four months shy of the date.

"Yes," Jorge told her, "that's what I want."

Even as he said the words, it intrigued him that he really, *really* meant them. Sure, he had always liked women—loved them—but he had to admit, even though it unnerved him a little, that he had never quite felt this way before.

In general, he was captivated by vivacious women who liked life in the fast lane. Women who knew that having any long-term designs on him would only be futile.

Until New Year's Eve.

This one was different, he thought, not for the first time. This one was not the kind of woman you enjoyed for an unspecified amount of time and then moved on from. Jane Gilliam was the kind of woman his mother would have called the marrying kind.

Jorge knew himself, knew that he had no desire to get married, to be tied down to one woman. But be that as it may, he couldn't seem to get himself to just walk away.

The coat he'd been left holding in his parents' restaurant could have easily been delivered to Jane in a number of ways, none of which involved his putting in an appearance. But he hadn't wanted to just ship the coat off to her. He'd wanted to bring it to her in person. And find out why she'd left the restaurant so abruptly.

More than that, he realized, he'd wanted to see her again.

He told himself that it was to prove that there'd just been something about that particular night that had attracted him to her—and now it was gone.

But seeing her, seeing that strange combination of vulnerability mixed with an endearing innocence and sense of wonder, was stirring something in him. Something that he couldn't quite identify.

Something, he thought, that made him a little uneasy. Maybe he should leave well enough alone and leave it nameless. Because, at bottom, it was something that had the potential to scare the hell out of him because he couldn't seem to exercise control over it. And he didn't like not being in control.

"Why?" Jane heard herself finally asking.

She was being stupid, she silently upbraided herself. Any other woman would have just eagerly absorbed the attention, however fleeting, of easily the best-looking man in Red Rock. By questioning she was almost guaranteed to chase him away.

And yet, she had to know his motives.

She liked things to make sense and this just didn't.

She was familiar with some of the women Jorge had been seen with and there was just no way she fit into that category. She was neither drop-dead gorgeous, nor the owner of a body whose curves could make a grown man weep.

She did have, Jane knew, a good heart, but that wasn't something that was visible to the naked eye and she was fairly certain that Jorge wasn't out to add a girl scout to his extensive collection of conquests.

"Why?" he repeated her question incredulously, not sure what she was asking.

"Yes." Summoning her courage, she decided to be direct. "Why do you want to see me again?"

No one had ever asked him that before. Every woman had just jumped at the chance. Jane was a challenge all right. "Because I'm attracted to you, Jane," he told her. "Isn't that why most men and women date one another?"

Date? He was asking to date her? As in seeing her more than once?

For one wild, wonderful moment, Jane felt as if she'd suddenly slipped into the Twilight Zone. Lost for words, she bit into the sweet cake she'd been holding in her hand. Her mouth full, she stalled for time, desperately trying to understand what was going on here.

She couldn't make herself believe that she'd hit the jackpot.

Maybe it was karma, something Isabella had

mentioned to her on several occasions. The young woman felt that life was a series of checks and balances. Isabella had told her more than once that someone as good as she was was definitely on track to be on the receiving end of something wonderful.

She figured that the New Year's Eve kiss had wiped that slate clean—until she'd overheard those two boys talking.

Jorge glanced at his watch. He was due at a meeting with a client soon. Besides, the receptionist had told him that Jane had someone to tutor in less than an hour. Even so, he felt a reluctance to get up and leave.

Standing up, Jorge extended his hand to her. She accepted it almost hesitantly. Somewhere in the back of his mind, it struck him that the feel of her hand in his seemed very right somehow. He tamped down the thought.

Still holding her hand, he pulled Jane up to her feet and wound up pulling her closely against him.

Sparks began to go off up and down her body, sending out alarms, quickening her pulse. He made no effort to put space between them. Instead, he just stood there, holding her. Making her warm.

And then her heart all but stopped as she watched him lower his head. Their lips met.

And Jane felt herself slipping into a dark, velvet-lined abyss.

Hardly aware of what she was doing, Jane laced her arms around Jorge's neck. Her body leaning into his, she kissed him back as if her very life depended on it.

And maybe it did.

Because if she hadn't kissed him back with such verve, she would have surely gone under for a third time and drowned in ecstasy.

All in all, she thought in her heart of hearts, that wouldn't be such a bad a way to go, dying with a smile on her lips.

"I guess I'd better be going," Jorge murmured, drawing back his head.

But even as he said it, he continued holding her, his hands resting on the swell of her hips. He could feel desire coursing through his body. She was arousing a hunger in him that couldn't be addressed at the moment.

But soon, he promised himself. And as soon as that happened, he knew that this attraction would fade.

It always did.

"You said you had students to tutor soon and I don't want you getting in trouble on my account."

Too late, she thought.

Jane searched her empty brain cavity for something to say. She'd never been a brilliant conversationalist, but until now, she'd been able to hold her own. That wasn't the case anymore.

"They should be here soon," she finally managed to get out.

Finally letting her go, Jorge bent down and quickly scooped up the plates and utensils, wrapping them inside the checkered tablecloth. Securing it, he dumped the whole thing into the picnic basket.

Jane heard the dishes clink against each other. Thinking that he might wind up breaking them, she cautioned, "Be careful."

He looked into her eyes, soft brown eyes that he'd discovered he could easily get lost in.

"I'm trying to be," Jorge told her honestly. But he wasn't all that sure how that was working out for him. Because if he were really being careful, he wouldn't have allowed his curiosity to bring him here. "Why don't you give me your home number and I'll give you a call?" he suggested.

Even she had heard that line before, Jane thought. She'd give him her number, but she wasn't going to hold her breath, waiting. He'd forget about calling her the minute he got into his car. Sooner, maybe.

But that was all right. This had been very, very nice while it had lasted.

Tearing a piece of paper from the spiral notebook on her desk, Jane wrote down her name and number, then added in parenthesis: the girl you kissed at midnight on New Year's Eve. Finished, she folded the sheet and handed it to him.

Taking the paper, Jorge unfolded it and read what she'd written. The smile that played on his lips was ever so slightly lopsided. He refolded the paper and slipped it into his pocket.

"You didn't have to write that down. I know who you are, Jane."

She lifted her shoulders in a quick shrug. "Just in case you come across that note sometime later and can't place the name," she explained casually.

He found her lack of ego refreshing and appealing. Some of the women he'd been with couldn't walk by a mirror without glancing at their reflection, checking to see that every hair was in place, that their makeup was picture-perfect, and that they were still as alluring as they had been an hour ago. In comparison, Jane seemed far more genuine.

"Even then I'll be able to place the name," he assured her.

She sincerely doubted it. She wasn't the kind of woman who left a lasting impression and she'd made her peace with that. "Thank you for the early lunch," she said.

Jorge gave her a slightly courtly bow and said, "My pleasure," just before he kissed her hand.

And then, as her heart launched into double time, he was gone.

But she had no time to savor the last hour or to even review a single sweet moment because suddenly the door opened again and the room was filled with every woman who worked at or volunteered at ReadingWorks. And every one of them was eager for information.

Harriet moved close to Jane, a wide grin on her face. "I guess you must have had a *really* nice lunch."

"Yes," Jane admitted, "I did." Her thoughts lingered on the feel of his lips moving over hers, stirring things inside her that had never even been touched before. No wonder he had such a following. The man was a fantastic kisser. "It was very nice."

Jane discovered that it was impossible to keep the smile both out of her voice and from her lips.

She still didn't have a clue what was going on but one kiss from Jorge and nothing else seemed to matter. At least, not for now.

This was not the time nor the place to daydream, she upbraided herself. They had work to do. The first of the students would be arriving any second.

"Workstations, ladies," Jane announced abruptly, calling a halt to any other personal questions that might be forthcoming.

She could hear cars pulling up in the parking lot. The first wave of students were being dropped off by their parents. It was time to stop obsessing about a man who was nothing more than a wonderful fantasy and turn her attention to something that actually had substance. Teaching children to read.

"Fine," Cecilia acknowledged with no small reluctance. "But don't even think about leaving without telling us everything that happened." Her eyes narrowed as she looked at Jane. "If you know what's good for you."

Nodding, Jane played along. She did know what was good for her. And it had nothing to do with Jorge Mendoza. But just for now, she could pretend that it actually did.

After all, what could it hurt?

"You, it could hurt you," Isabella insisted later that evening over the phone. It seemed that rumors were already making the rounds and, concerned,

Isabella had called her friend the moment she'd heard. Jane, Isabella was convinced, was far too innocent for the likes of her cousin. "Don't get me wrong, I love Jorge. Every woman over the age of eighteen months loves Jorge, but that doesn't mean that he's the kind of guy you should fall for. That would be a huge mistake, Jane," she cautioned. "He'll break your heart. He won't mean it but he can't help himself. He's just one of those guys who can't stay put."

"Don't worry," Jane tried to sound nonchalant. "I'm aware of his reputation."

"Good. Keep that in mind."

Sitting down in the easy chair she'd splurged on when she'd moved into this apartment, Jane kicked off her shoes and then raised her feet. It had been a long day. "What I don't know is why he wants to go out with me."

There was silence on the other end of the line, as if Isabella were searching for an explanation. "Because maybe, just maybe, he's growing up and he realizes that all the other women he's been with are just bimbos. Trust me, none of them are good enough to walk on the same side of the street as you."

She laughed softly. Isabella was very sweet. "I don't think that walking is what Jorge had in mind with them."

She heard Isabella sigh. "That's just it. He's a lover of women." Because they were cousins, albeit distant, she tried to give him the benefit of the doubt.

"I don't want you getting charmed by him until he can prove that he's finally matured."

Too late, Jane thought. She'd already been charmed. Right down to her toes. And dazzled as well. The only thing she had going for her was that she knew that it was only going to last until the next beautiful woman caught his eye. She was just a filler, a way for him to kill time.

But that didn't mean she couldn't enjoy herself. And she'd decided right after he'd kissed her today that she fully intended to.

Chapter Eight

In a hurry because traffic had made her late getting home, Jane had just slipped one arm into her coat sleeve when her cell phone rang. Taking a second to inhale deeply—she could swear she still detected a hint of Jorge's cologne on the wool—Jane dug into her purse to retrieve the phone.

Slipping the other sleeve on, she answered the call, interrupting the second chorus of a popular Elvis classic that was her ringtone of choice.

"Hello?"

A deep voice chuckled. "You sound breathless. Did I interrupt something?"

Jorge.

The sound of his voice brought everything to a

screeching halt—except for her stomach, which was in the middle of flipping over. It took her a couple of seconds to pull herself together. He was actually calling her. When she'd given Jorge her phone number, she'd never expected him to use it.

"No, you didn't interrupt anything." She didn't sound very convincing, Jane thought, not even to her own ear.

"Good. Listen, I was just in the neighborhood and wondered if you'd mind if I dropped by."

Her pulse scrambled, even as disappointment washed over her. She would have liked nothing more than to say yes and have him come over, but there were people—children—waiting for her. And children remembered promises that were broken.

She had.

"I would really love to see you," she said without any attempt at guile. And then regret filled her voice as she took hold of the doorknob and turned it. "But I was just on my way—"

The last word stuck in her throat. There, leaning against her doorjamb, phone pressed to his ear and a spectacular smile gracing his sensual lips, was Jorge.

"Out," Jane said, finally managing to get the last word out.

Closing his phone, Jorge straightened as he slipped it back into the hip pocket of his jeans. It was close to six o'clock in the evening and he'd been pretty certain he'd find her home.

Just not looking like this.

His eyes swept over her, taking in her outfit and the fact that her hair was confined in two playful pigtails. Amusement played on his lips.

"And just where is it that you're going?" he asked. "Clog-dancing?"

Her coat was hanging open. Beneath it was a wide, colorful skirt and a black vest laced up the front worn over a gleaming white peasant blouse. She had on knee-high white socks and a pair of Mary Janes.

Was she role-playing, he wondered, his interest definitely aroused. Was there a kinky side to this otherwise shy, bookish woman that he hadn't even suspected?

Just went to show that no one was as uncomplicated as they seemed.

"No." She looked down at her feet. "These are shoes, not clogs." Realizing that her answer didn't begin to address the question in his eyes and wary of where his imagination might be taking him, she hurried to explain. "I'm reading *Heidi* to the kids in Red Rock Memorial Hospital." He was still looking at the outfit she had on. The interest in his eyes intensified. "Dressing up like one of the main characters makes the story more vivid for them."

His grin went directly under her skin, raising her body temperature. "Tell me when you get around to reading them the story of Lady Godiva."

To his further amusement and delight, he saw a blush begin to rise up her throat, coloring her cheeks. He didn't think women blushed anymore. Certainly not the ones he typically dated.

Jane cleared her throat, looking away. "That's not on the list."

"Too bad." His eyes pinned her in place. "Maybe you could give me a private reading sometime."

C'mon, Jane, the kids are waiting. Get a grip. You can go to fantasyland some other time.

"I don't think you really need to be stimulated or motivated," she told him, those being just some of the reasons she volunteered her time at the children's ward in the hospital.

Right now, Jorge thought, he was plenty stimulated. He had no idea that "cute" could be such a turn-on. "You look very Heidi-ish," he finally said.

She'd never thought of Heidi as being sensual before. She did now. "Thank you," Jane murmured.

Twirling one of her pigtails around his finger, he kept his eyes on her face. "Sure I can't get you to postpone this?"

She sincerely doubted that she'd ever been so tempted to go back on her word in her life. But she *had* given her word and all she had to think about were all the times that her parents broke promises they had made to her, or worse, forgot that they had made them at all, and that made up her mind for her.

It killed her to do it, but Jane flashed an apologetic smile and shook her head. "I can't. I gave my word. They're waiting for me."

"This is new for me," he had to admit, "losing out to a bunch of kids."

"Hospitalized kids," she emphasized.

"Hospitalized kids," he repeated dutifully. And then he really surprised her. "Mind if I tag along?"

The air was cold and she quickly secured a button, pushing it through its hole before locking the door behind her. He was kidding, right?

"You want to come to the hospital with me?" she asked incredulously.

"Yes."

She tried to picture him in the ward, surrounded by small children. It wasn't easy. "Why?"

He wasn't used to being questioned as to his motives. She was definitely keeping him on his toes. "I never read *Heidi* as a kid."

Now *that* she believed. "I'm in the middle of the book," she warned.

If that was meant to make him change his mind about coming along, it failed. "Don't worry, I'll catch up," he assured her. "I've been told I'm bright for my age," he teased.

She was out of excuses and if she was being honest with herself, she liked the idea that he wanted to come with her. It made him seem more human to her.

"All right," she agreed, "if you're sure you want to do this. My car's parked over here." She nodded in the general direction of the carport and then led the way to her space.

Jorge kept pace with her and then watched the way the wind played with the ends of her hair as she unlocked her side of the car. Opening the door, she hit the lock release. His door was opened.

"Is this part of your job, too?" he asked as he got into the small, economical foreign vehicle. "Reading to kids in hospitals?"

"No." Leaving her purse on the floor between her and the door, she put on her seat belt. "I wanted to do something meaningful and this was the only thing I could think of—entertaining the kids at the hospital by reading to them."

His seat belt was giving him trouble. He had to extend it twice before he could get it to fit into the slot.

"Wouldn't it be easier just to donate a couple of video games and maybe a secondhand game console?" he suggested.

"Easier, maybe," she agreed looking over her shoulder as she pulled out of her spot, "but not nearly as rewarding." Books had always been her saving grace, her safe place to go when things became difficult to deal with. "Books spark the imagination."

He thought of some of his friends' kids. They spent hours glued to a television set, their fingers flying across a keypad. "So do video games."

She supposed video games had their place, but she had never cared for them. "Most video games are about blowing things up. Books build minds."

There was a note of passion in her voice, as if she were defending old friends. "Bet you read a lot as a kid," he said.

She'd taken a lot of teasing for that, but that had helped her develop a tougher outer shell. "Anything I could get my hands on," she confirmed. "I loved to escape into stories." It wasn't until the word was out that she realized her mistake.

"What were you escaping from?" Jorge asked, his curiosity aroused.

If she'd had more time, she would have come up with some vague, acceptable story. But the question was here and now. She had no choice but to fall back on the truth. "Parents who yelled at each other and ignored me."

He hadn't anticipated that kind of an answer. His parents had always been there for him, even when he hadn't deserved it. Sometimes he forgot that he was one of the lucky ones and that not everyone grew up with a support system to fall back on.

Not that he ever did, he thought, but it was still nice to know it was there if he needed it.

"Must have been rough," he sympathized.

She shrugged, glad that she had an excuse to avoid his eyes. The last thing she wanted to see there was pity.

"Other people had it worse." She suppressed a sigh. There was no changing the past. "They were just two people who should have never gotten married. To anyone," she added. Her father had been completely into his work and her mother had been completely into herself. They didn't need outsiders in their lives and they certainly didn't need to be responsible for a child. "I used to wonder why they got married in the first place."

Jorge thought of all the times he'd seen his father sneak up behind his mother and steal a kiss or nuzzle her. He'd grown up thinking that all parents loved each other and demonstrated their affection.

"Did you ever ask them?"

"I asked my mother once," she recalled. "She said it seemed like a good idea at the time." A rueful smile curved her lips. "One of the longest conversations I ever had with her."

"Do you have any brothers or sisters?" Having someone sympathetic to turn to could help take the edge off rejection.

Jane kept her eyes on the road, even as her mind revisited the past. Even with the distance of time, it was painful to recall. She shook her head. "One mistake was enough for them."

"Is that what they told you?" Jorge could feel his temper suddenly materializing out of nowhere, flaring and aimed at people he wouldn't have recognized if he tripped over them on the street. How could people say something that hurtful to any kid, let alone their own?

"In a way," she recalled. "When I was six, one of the girls at school bragged about getting a new baby sister over the summer. I came home and asked my mother if we could get one and she looked at me for a long time and then said that when people made mistakes, they were supposed to learn from them, not make another one." She could feel his eyes on her and she flushed, glancing at him. "I didn't understand what she meant at the time, but I figured it out later."

The sadness in her voice was hard to miss. But there was no condemnation.

"And you're not bitter?" he asked in amazement. A background like that was perfect for producing loners and serial killers, yet here she was, sweet and generous to a fault, working at a job that he knew for a fact paid very little, just because she wanted to help children.

"Wouldn't change anything if I was," she theorized. "Besides, they did the best they could."

Jane's reasoning eluded him. "How do you figure that?"

"I never went hungry." *At least, not for food,* she thought. "I had shelter, clothes and a library card." Mentioning the last item made her smile fondly. It was one of her best childhood memories. "My father took me to get it when I was seven. The only outing I remember with him, actually," she confessed.

There were no picnics, no trips to amusement parks, no family vacations in her past. She grew up in a house with two self-involved adults, very much alone.

Maybe the man was a workaholic, Jorge thought. "What did your father do for a living?"

"He was an engineer. Aerospace," she added. A sigh accompanied her next statement. "He was away a lot. NASA had him on speed dial," she said with a small laugh. "I think he just used work to get away from my mother." And inadvertently, her, she added silently.

"And your mother?"

Her mother.

There were no fond memories when she thought of the woman, no nostalgia, no sense of any connection at all. Her mother was just a beautiful woman who happened to have the same address as she did.

"My mother peaked at nineteen. She was Miss Texas in the Miss USA Pageant that year. She came in third and said that she was cheated." Jane shrugged, as if she wasn't sure whether or not to give that claim any credence. She did know that, as far as looks went, she had always been a huge disappointment to her mother. "After that, she became a professional shopper."

"She shopped for other people?" He'd heard of those, but thought they were generally employed by celebrities who had trouble going out in public. There was no one like that around here.

"Not other people. She shopped strictly for herself." She remembered feeling hopeful the first few times she recalled her mother coming home with shopping bags full of things. But there was never anything in them for her. And after a while, she stopped hoping. "She was only happy when she was buying things. That was why my parents argued rather than talked to each other," she explained. "My father claimed that she spent money faster than he earned it."

"And did she?"

The short laugh had a sad sound to it. "Absolutely."

Making a left turn, Jane pulled onto the hospital compound. She hadn't realized that she'd talked all the way here. It certainly hadn't been her intention to go on and on like that.

"Well, there you have it." She tried to make a joke of the fact that she'd revealed so much, "My whole life story. Not exactly a page-turner, was it?" There was a parking structure straight ahead. She drove into it and parked her vehicle in the first space she could find. Turning off the engine, she turned to look at him. She was surprised that Jorge hadn't tried to jump out of the car. "I didn't mean to bore you."

"I wasn't bored," he protested. If anything, he'd gained new respect for her.

"Now you're just being polite." She released her seat belt. "Shoelaces have more exciting backstories than I do."

Jorge grinned. The novelty of a modest woman hadn't grown old yet. "I don't usually talk to shoe-laces," he told her.

She laughed shortly. "You know what I mean."

"Yes, I do," he acknowledged, "and you're wrong." He saw her raise her eyebrows in a silent question. "I don't find you dull or boring."

This bet that Jorge had going—the one that involved her—it had to be for quite a lot of money, she thought. She couldn't conceive of any other reason for him to be so accommodating, so nice to her.

Picking up her purse, she then leaned over the seat, reaching into the back for a large book whose edges were gilded in gold. On the front cover was a young woman who, at first glance, Jorge thought, bore a remarkable resemblance to Jane. A second look made him realize that it was the hairstyle and the clothes that were responsible for the likeness.

However they both had a fresh-faced appeal, he noted, although Jane was obviously older. But definitely not by much. She could have easily passed for a schoolgirl.

Jane got out of the car. Waiting until he followed suit, she hit the security lock. They walked toward the hospital's main entrance.

She tried to give him one last out. "You know, the hospital has a really good cafeteria. The food's not as good as what your father prepares, but the coffee's decent. You could wait there if you wanted to."

Reaching the entrance, he waited for her to go through the electronic doors first. "Why would I want to do that? I came along to see you in action, not to drink watered-down cafeteria coffee."

"It's not watered down," she assured him. "As a matter of fact, it's pretty strong. Designed to keep sleepy interns on their feet."

In action.

He said he wanted to see her in action. Somehow, she'd never thought of those words being associated with her. *Action* referred to the dynamic people in the world. She wasn't dynamic, she was just a person who did whatever needed doing.

Yet Jane had to admit that a part of her was glad she wasn't able to talk him out of coming to listen to her read.

Another part was nervous for the same reason.

"Okay," she said. "Just remember, this was your idea."

"I'll remember," he assured her, striding to keep up with her as she wove her way through the ground floor to the elevators on the far side of the building.

Jane hurried out the moment the silver doors parted on the fourth floor children's ward. And narrowly avoided crashing into an older woman dressed in immaculate hospital whites.

Rather than be upset at the near collision, the woman offered up half a prayer of thanksgiving. "Oh, thank God you're here," she cried. "I thought you weren't coming. I would have had a rebellion on my hands." She sounded completely serious.

"We had a little traffic," Jane explained. By now, the nurse had stopped looking relieved and had focused the sum of her attention on the man directly beside her. "Adrienne, this Jorge Mendoza. He told me he's never read *Heidi* and wanted to hear the story."

The nurse's eyes were all but shining as they skimmed over Jorge. Had there been more time, there might have been questions, or at least inane conversation. But Adrienne's first order of business was to maintain peace and that was giving every indication of disappearing if she didn't get Jane into the room—fast.

"You'd better hurry and get out there, Heidi.

Some of those kids have been waiting for over twenty-five minutes," Adrienne told her.

"Twenty-five minutes?" Jane echoed. She shrugged out of her coat, draping it on her arm. "I thought we agreed that they weren't supposed to gather together in the lounge until I got here."

"We agreed but they didn't," the nurse corrected. "They all started coming into the lounge on their own right after dinner. I don't think you realize how much they look forward to you reading to them or what a big hit you are."

Silent up until now, Jorge put in his two cents. "Jane has this tendency to underestimate herself," he confided to the nurse.

Jane caught the look in the head nurse's eyes as they shifted from Jorge to her. She could swear she could almost hear the woman applauding her.

As if she had anything to do with Jorge's being here, Jane thought.

But there was no time to protest or ponder over whatever accolades the woman was silently awarding her. She had a pint-sized audience eagerly waiting to hear the further adventures of a plucky little girl who lived in the Alps with her grandfather.

Leaving her purse on a chair, along with her coat, Jane picked up her book and walked into the next room.

The walls were decorated with paintings done by patients and the room was littered with toys, some worn, some fairly new, all scattered about on small tables.

The children broke into a cheer when she walked in. Some were sitting on the floor, others took their places at the miniature tables. A couple of the children were in wheelchairs.

"Hi, kids," she greeted them cheerily. "Sorry I'm late."

She sounded, Jorge thought as he took his place by the doorway, like a completely different person than the woman he'd met on New Year's Eve. Confident, poised and full of fun.

Definitely a woman he wanted to get closer to.

Chapter Nine

For the most part, children were not among the vast number of people with whom Jorge had daily contact. He didn't know how to talk to them or what to expect when he was around them.

So it was with a degree of interest and no small amount of fascination that he watched the group within the lounge become captivated almost from the moment that Jane began to read.

And they remained that way, spellbound by something he would have bet money should have bored them to tears. After all, the story of *Heidi* was a gentle, peaceful one, relying on emotions more than drama. As far as he knew, nothing exploded, nothing even made a loud noise.

But for more than an hour, all there was was the sound of Jane's voice as she provided both the book's narrative and the voices of all the different characters in the timeworn classic. As he watched and listened, Jane became Heidi, then Peter, the goat herder, and, most delightfully, she became Grandfather, in all the blustery glory that eventually gave way to a loving man.

There was no other sound in the room, no whispers to distract the others from story. Every pair of eyes, and that included those of the nurses, were unwaveringly on Jane as she breathed life into every word, every nuance, vividly creating scene after scene for her small audience.

The woman was definitely gifted, he thought. He would never have guessed that she had this talent. And when she finished for the evening, he was almost as disappointed as the children.

"Can't you do a little more?" one of the girls begged. Her eyes were bright blue and she had a head full of golden curls.

Jane smiled, but she shook her head. The book remained closed, a bookmark marking where she would start reading the next time. "It's late and someone has to get to bed."

"But I'm not tired," the little girl protested, ending her sentence with a pronounced pout.

"I meant me, Faith," Jane told the girl with a laugh. She went through the motions of an exaggerated yawn. "I've had a very long day and I'm pretty tired." Enthusiasm entered her voice as she continued. The woman was a born storyteller, Jorge thought. "But just think, that gives us another day to get together and see what happens to Heidi now that she's in the big city."

"Will you come tomorrow?" another little girl begged. She looked frailer than the first girl and had a red and yellow bandanna tied around her head.

Jane smiled at her as she gently ran her hand along the girl's bandanna. Ordinarily she came by twice, sometimes even three times a week. She'd already put in her three days. But how could she find it in her heart to say no to someone who was obviously so much braver than she was?

"I'll come tomorrow, Betty," she promised.

Several of the younger children, including, to Jorge's surprise, the boys, cheered.

Herding the children together, the nurses began to empty the lounge. Jane waved and said a few words to each and every child who left the room. Only once they were gone she picked up her book and, holding it to her chest, glance in the direction where she'd last seen Jorge.

She half expected him to be gone.

But he wasn't.

He was right where he had been for the last seventy-three minutes, leaning against the doorjamb on the other side of the room. Now that the children were gone, he crossed to her. Jane attempted to read the expression on his face. While open and friendly, it still gave nothing away.

There was another layer to the man, she thought,

one that he kept private and under wraps. She couldn't help wondering what he was like, deep down inside, when he wasn't being the extremely seductive Jorge Mendoza.

"You are a very interesting person, Jane Gilliam." He was close enough to whisper the words. Why did everything that came out of his mouth make her heart beat faster? She had a feeling that he could make her pulse spike simply by describing the weather.

She couldn't guess what was going through his mind. Was he being sarcastic? She'd never thought of herself as particularly interesting. "Because I dress up to read books to kids?"

That was part of it, but it wasn't what he really meant. "Because you give so much of yourself. Tell me, after you give all that away, is there anything left over for you?"

She didn't feel herself particularly depleted. "Oh, there's lots left over for me," she assured him.

This volunteer work was only a small part of her life, although she was thinking about expanding it. Red Rock Memorial Hospital wasn't the only place where children were forced to remain while they underwent treatment for conditions they didn't understand. The fact that these treatments made them better—most of the time—compensated for the discomfort and loneliness they experienced. The nurses could only do so much and she wanted to help.

Jane firmly believed that as her diminutive listeners became involved in the worlds she verbally created for them, these small patients were transported to lands they'd never been to before, and that helped alleviate their loneliness. And, for a little while, their fears.

"Have you had dinner yet?" Jorge asked. As if on cue, her stomach rumbled and he grinned. "I'll take that as a no."

The sounds coming from her stomach embarrassed her. There hadn't been time to eat. "You don't have to keep feeding me," she told him.

He studied her for a moment. She fidgeted ever so slightly. "You're an independent woman, aren't you?"

She hadn't thought of herself that way, but she realized that he was right. Independent women probably weren't his type, but it wasn't in her to lie. "I've had to be."

To her surprise, he nodded as he took in the information.

"Fine. I have nothing against independent women." The grin made her weak—hunger had nothing to do with it. "And to prove it, I'll even let you pay."

A laugh escaped her lips as she reached for her coat. "I'm not *that* independent." She had to watch every penny if she wanted to continue the work she was doing.

"No problem," Jorge assured her as he moved behind her and helped her slip the coat on. "I like playing the man."

He didn't have to play at it, she thought, enjoying

the way his hands felt on her shoulders even through the coat. Jorge *was* the man. *All* man.

"Do you mind if I go home and change first?" she asked as they walked out of the building.

There were far fewer people around now as they crossed to the parking structure where she'd left the car. Evening had descended, weaving shadows in and out of the landscape.

"If you want to," he answered. "Although I think you kind of look cute in knee socks." She felt his eyes sweep over her as they reached her car. "Actually, if you stay in that outfit, someone might call the police to have me arrested for endangering the morals of a minor."

Getting behind the wheel, Jane glanced at her reflection in the rearview mirror before buckling up. "I don't look that young," she protested. Although maybe the pigtails did cut a few years off her age, she decided.

She looked like a teenager in his opinion. "Let's put it this way," he said, his seat belt clicking into place, "in that outfit you don't run the risk of having Boy Scouts fight over which one gets to help you across the street—they'd be fighting over which one gets to kiss you at the movies."

He had a silver tongue all right, she thought, turning her key in the ignition. But she was a realist and while his words sounded pretty, she knew it was all just empty flattery. She wasn't the kind anyone would ever fight over.

"You must know some pretty desperate Boy Scouts," she commented as the engine came to life.

"You know, you shouldn't do that," Jorge told her seriously.

She thought he was referring to the car stalling out. "Do what?"

"Sell yourself short like that."

"I don't sell myself short," she told him. Looking both ways, she slowly inched out of the space. "I know exactly what I am and what I'm not."

"And what are you?" he asked, curious to hear what she had placed in the plus column.

She made a right at the end of the winding road, leaving the hospital compound. "I'm hardworking, generous, fairly intelligent and very loyal to my friends."

"You forgot kind to small animals and children."

She heard the smile in his voice, and it coaxed one from her in kind. "That goes without saying."

"And what aren't you?" he pressed.

"Pretty," she answered simply, mentally putting a barrier between herself and the word, the way she always did.

That smacked of an insult—and a deep wound. "Who told you that?"

She shrugged as she merged the vehicle into the main thoroughfare that led away from the hospital and eventually brought her to her apartment complex. "No one had to tell me that. I have mirrors in my apartment."

It wasn't a mirror that had made her feel this way, he thought. It was someone who mattered. "They need to be replaced, because you're not seeing what I see."

She wished he'd stop that, stopped saying all those nice things that weren't true. Because she was liable to start believing him and then she'd really be setting herself up for a fall.

"My mother told me I was plain," she finally said. "It really seemed to bother her that I wasn't pretty." She spared him a quick glance before focusing back on the road. The full moon looked as if it were traveling with her. "Mothers aren't supposed to lie to their children."

"They're not supposed to, no, but not every mother should have been a mother," he reminded her. Hers certainly didn't win any prizes, he added silently. "Maybe yours was jealous."

"Of me?" Jane asked incredulously just before she laughed. Really laughed.

It had a nice sound, he thought, even if it was at her own expense.

"Of you," he repeated. "A lot of 'beauty queens' are very shallow and very jealous of anyone who might steal the spotlight from them. Especially as they get older. Trust me, I've known more than my share of those." Women who saw lines in the mirror that weren't there, who were afraid of getting a day older, a day beyond their prime.

He didn't sound as if he liked those women very much. "If that's what you think of them, why did you hang around them so much?"

When he'd been younger, there'd been more than his share of older women, women who were drawn to his sensuality as well as his youth. "Maybe that's why I'm not hanging around them anymore."

But you will be. Once you win your bet or get tired of your charade, you'll be back with those beautiful, vapid women, she thought.

And the thought filled her with a sadness that took more than a moment to shake.

"You know," Jane said twenty minutes later as she unlocked her apartment door, "If you've changed your mind about going out to eat, that's okay."

He'd never known a woman who constantly presented him with avenues of escape. Didn't she want to go out with him?

"I haven't changed my mind," he told her. "If anything, I'm hungrier." His eyes met hers. "How about you?"

She wasn't hungry as much as she was walking on air. Every time he looked at her like that, she became airborne. It was a struggle to remain grounded. Anchored. She kept reminding herself that none of this was what it seemed and that as long as she just enjoyed herself and didn't get carried away, it was going to be all right.

But it wasn't easy.

"I'll just be a minute," she promised, shedding her coat as she hurried toward her bedroom. She tossed her coat onto the sofa as she passed by it.

He saw her bedroom door close and for a moment, he felt a strong urge to open it and follow her inside. But he was fairly certain that if he did, it would spook her and he didn't want to do that. Didn't want to drive her away or traumatize her.

The winning over of Ms. Jane Gilliam was going to take time. The very thought intrigued him because he'd never had to coax a woman before. That he did, he supposed, was part of the attraction he felt. He had to admit that he'd never taken time to really get to know the woman behind the face and body before. Ordinarily his goal had always been gratification—both his and that of the woman he was with.

The latter had always been part and parcel of the deal. That way it worked out to everyone's mutual benefit. But this time around it was different. Different in a way that he didn't quite understand. But he meant to. And right now, there was nowhere else he wanted to be.

Less than five minutes later, the bedroom door opened.

Had she changed her mind?

Or was that a silent invitation for him to enter?

Jorge took exactly one step toward the bedroom before Jane came out, wearing a simple black pencil skirt and a powder blue pullover. Taking a complete inventory in less time than it took to say the phrase, he found his gaze lingering on her legs. Did she realize that she had killer legs? Probably not, he decided.

"That was fast. Most women I know—including my sisters," he added purposely so she wouldn't think he was just comparing her to the women he'd gone out with, "take that long just to reapply their lipstick."

She'd always been able to get ready at a moment's

notice. It evolved from a sense of knowing she'd be left behind if she kept either of her parents waiting the few times that they actually took her someplace with them.

"Not much to fuss with," she told him. "Besides, I was afraid you'd change your mind if I took too long." She'd almost said, "come to your senses," but she'd managed to stop herself just in time. "Are we going to your parents' restaurant again?"

He heard the barely suppressed note of eagerness in her voice. "I'd rather not." She slipped on her coat before he could help her with it. So he opened the door instead. "Unless you like eating with an audience."

Crossing the threshold, she looked at him, puzzled. "I don't understand."

He waited as she locked the door.

"Most evenings, my mother's there to help out. She has a wonderful memory." Whether Jane knew it or not, she was exactly what his mother would have chosen for him. "She sees you with me and I guarantee she'll take it as a sign that her prayers have been answered."

She'd never thought of herself as the answer to anyone's prayer. The last guy who'd unceremoniously dumped her just before New Year's had made that abundantly clear.

At the risk of sounding dumb, she said, "I still don't understand."

He led the way to guest parking, where he'd left his sports car.

"My mother is a wonderful woman who has what she feels are very simple wishes. She wants to see all of her children married—and she's willing to move heaven and earth—and everything in between—for that to happen. My sisters now are all taken care of, so my mother concentrates all her efforts on getting my older brother, Roberto, and me, married off."

As long as she was on her own and not a drain, her mother didn't care how she lived her life. "You should appreciate that your mother cares so much about your happiness."

Hitting the security lock, he opened the passenger door for her.

"I love my mother." His eyes lowered as she slid her legs in. "But her definition of happiness is not necessarily mine."

She waited until he got in on his side. "Meaning you never intend to get married?"

That sounded as if it was carved in stone. He shook his head.

"Meaning I don't intend to get married now. There's always tomorrow," he added, letting her in on his private philosophy.

Glancing at her before he pulled out of the parking spot, he noted that the smile on her lips had more than a hint of sadness to it.

"Not always," she told him. "My father always thought he'd have all the time in the world to do what he wanted to do 'tomorrow.' But for him, tomorrow didn't come."

Jorge read between the lines. "How old was he when he died?"

"Forty-two."

And although she had never managed to make her father proud of her the way she so desperately wanted him to be, she still missed him a great deal. Struggling for a moment, she managed to tamp down the melancholy feelings that were rushing through her.

He'd done it again. This was the second time she'd done this in the space of one evening.

Jane looked at Jorge ruefully. "How is it that I keep pouring out my soul to you?"

"Maybe I'm just in the right place at the right time," he suggested. "Besides, I like that you let me in like that." And he did.

Jorge decided not to tell Jane that most of his conversations with women revolved around vapid, empty subjects. That he hadn't dated them for their minds or for the desire to have a stimulating, challenging exchange of ideas.

Certainly none of those women had ever donated her time to do something meaningful. Money, yes, time, definitely not.

He made a right turn at the end of the complex. "So, Heidi," he teased. "What are you in the mood for tonight?"

She knew he was asking her about food, but from out of nowhere a single word shot through her brain. *You.*

She was only grateful that she managed to keep

her mouth shut. Otherwise she would have been so mortified she doubted if she would have ever recovered.

"I'll leave that up to you," she told him, having no real preference as long as she was with him. "I'm easy," she added.

The moment the phrase came out, she turned a bright shade of pink.

"I mean—"

He laughed as he eased onto the brake as the light turned red. "Don't get so flustered, Heidi. I know what you meant."

But even so, the phrase she'd used couldn't help but fuel some pretty wicked fantasies in his brain....

Chapter Ten

Several hours later, they were back at Jane's door.

Jorge waited as she looked through her purse, searching for her house key.

It had been an interesting evening for him. He'd gotten to watch her perform for the pint-size patients at the hospital, and then he'd spent an enjoyable hour and a half at the restaurant, talking to her.

Just talking.

Not planning a seduction, nor being confident that this was merely the second act, to be followed by an evening of lovemaking. He was simply sharing a meal and conversation, enjoying Jane's company more than he'd anticipated.

It was a little, he thought, like watching a flower

unfold during one of those nature programs that his mother liked to watch.

Jane was becoming less shy and more animated. He really liked the way her eyes lit up when she talked about something that captured her passion.

And he was surprised that her conversation touched on such a diversity of subjects. For such an initially soft-spoken person, it occurred to him that Jane had a huge frame of reference. She was able to intelligently discuss classical literature and popular music, as well as advances in medicine and technology, among other things.

He began to think that somewhere along the line, the petite woman had somehow committed an encyclopedia to memory.

"I just remember what I read," she'd told him, looking pleased that he'd noticed her intelligence.

"Everything?" he asked in amazement.

Sure, he'd heard about people who could retain things to such a degree, but he'd never encountered anyone like that. For him, studying in school had always been a chore. But then, he had been a rebel. He had never liked being forced to stay in an enclosed area. As far as he was concerned, life was a huge schoolhouse and he learned far more by experience than he ever had by reading.

Jane, he'd come to realize, was his exact opposite. And even though there was that old saying about opposites attracting, he'd never given it any credence until now.

"Everything," she'd answered. He could see that

she was watching him to gauge his reaction. She'd probably been teased about how smart she was, he thought. Some men were intimidated by intelligent women. He'd never had that problem. "I just have to read it once and I remember it."

"Must be pretty crowded in there," he'd speculated, lightly tapping her forehead with his finger.

She'd smiled at him then, that blushing smile he found endearing because it was so honest, so devoid of any guile.

He'd taken his time with dinner because he'd known instinctively that once he brought her to her door, that would be the end of the evening. He wasn't the kind to force himself on a woman—he'd never had to, but even so, that would never have been his style. And, as he had already come to realize, Jane was in a class by herself. She wasn't the kind who topped off a night out by a night in.

But now that he was standing here, about to say good-night and take his leave, Jorge really didn't want to. As much as he didn't want to push, to have her do anything that was out of character for her, he didn't want to just walk away.

Jane could feel her heart doing a little dance in her chest. Feelings were madly scrambling through her, at war with her own code of ethics.

Common sense kept telling her there was no future with this man. Today, tomorrow, next week, whenever he tired of the chase—or won the bet— Jorge would vanish, move on to the next woman who caught his fancy or became a challenge to him.

And she would be left behind with a huge hole in her heart.

She knew herself, knew that if she let these mounting feelings within her lead her astray, she'd only be hurt that much more when the inevitable breakup came.

And yet…she wanted him. Wanted him to want *her*.

Was she crazy?

Or simply just that attracted to him?

Jane opened the door and then turned around to face him. It took her a second to find her voice.

"Thank you for a lovely surprise," she told him. Jorge cocked his head, as if he didn't quite follow her line of thinking. "I didn't expect you to drop by," she explained. "And I certainly didn't think you'd be willing to actually come along and put up with story time at the hospital."

The corners of his generous mouth curved. "And miss seeing you in that outfit?" he asked. "Not a chance."

He ran his hands along her arms, struggling to keep himself in check. He knew damn well that all he had to do was kiss her, *really* kiss her and he could seduce her. It wasn't that he thought of himself as irresistible. There was no ego or self-flattery at work here—he just knew what he was capable of.

He also knew that while the seduction would most likely be excruciatingly sweet, the guilt that would follow—and the pain he would cause—would be difficult to deal with. Nothing was worth that.

"I'd like to see you again, Jane," he told her and saw surprise blossom in her eyes.

She almost asked why. Was there more to the bet than she knew about? Had it escalated? Did it come in parts? Was the end goal to take her to bed?

No, she couldn't make herself believe that Jorge would actually be party to something like that. Kissing her on a dare or a bet was one thing, but the other—no, not him. She didn't care what his reputation was. If he *were* like that kind of man, he would have already made his move, would have attempted to get her into bed.

But he hadn't pushed.

Maybe, she mused, that was his strategy. She wasn't sure. All she knew was that she didn't want to give up seeing Jorge as long as possible—on her terms. He made her feel special, even if he confused everything inside her.

Maybe she was supposed to sound blasé, Jane thought, like the women she knew he was accustomed to. But that wouldn't be her and ultimately, if she tried to sound like one of those women, that would be lying. Because she wasn't feeling blasé.

Excited was a far better word for what she was experiencing.

"I'd like that," she told him.

"Me, too."

Framing her face in his hands, he brought his mouth down to hers and ignited a skyful of fireworks inside her head. She threaded her arms around his neck as much for support as for contact. The kiss deepened and she did her best to return it in kind. She didn't want to just be on the receiving end of this lightning in a bottle. More than anything, she was desperately trying to give him a reason to return.

To want to kiss her again not because it was part of a bet, but because he enjoyed it.

She had no idea how sweet she tasted, how inflamed she made him, Jorge thought. Or how much he wanted to push open that door that she'd unlocked. How much he wanted to scoop her up into his arms and carry her to her bedroom to make love with her.

And how hard it was not to.

So instead, he savored the kiss, letting it go on as long it was safe to. Just before his control cracked, Jorge broke contact.

There was pure mischief in his eyes as they looked into hers.

"Sleep well, *querida*," he murmured just before he turned on his heel and walked away.

Querida.

Beloved?

He'd called her "beloved"? Her hammering heart went into double time as she sighed and slipped inside her apartment, locking the door and then leaning against it, her eyes fluttering shut as she relived every fiber-shaking moment of his lips on hers.

She hugged herself. Life had never felt so wonderful and even if it was fleeting, right here, right now, this moment was hers to savor.

* * *

Jorge's footsteps on the asphalt seemed to echo into the silence of the night as he walked back to his sports car. A part of him couldn't believe that he was actually walking away from Jane. She was so very ripe for the taking—and he'd wanted her.

But he had to admit that this route—if it turned out to be a route—was far more intriguing and enticing. He'd never held out before, never not availed himself of what was right there before him.

Never wanted the chase, the pursuit, to continue before.

Never met a woman like Jane before, he thought, walking toward guest parking. She was a woman of substance, of integrity. She was a woman he wanted to get to know from head to toe.

Slowly.

Maybe he was just bored with his life, Jorge reasoned. Bored and looking for something different, some way to divert himself.

Or maybe, he thought as he unlocked the driver's side of his vehicle and got into it, he was in over his head. Maybe he should get out now, before something happened that he couldn't foresee. Or even worse, not be able to control.

The thought haunted him all the way home.

Walking into the house, Jorge headed straight for the small bar he kept in the living room. He reached into the cabinet without looking and took out a bottle of his favorite whiskey.

Jorge poured two fingers' worth into the chunky glass that stood on the counter. Downing the drink quickly, he briefly entertained the idea of another shot, then decided against it.

He didn't need to numb himself—he needed advice. He needed to talk to someone he respected. That didn't leave a large pool to choose from.

Although he dearly loved each of his sisters, he knew without being told that they would all be taking Jane's side of it. They might love him, but they were women first.

Damn, he wasn't sure *what* it was that he wanted to hear.

For a moment he thought about calling his father, then quickly abandoned that idea. Talking to him wouldn't help, not about something like this. It had been more than forty years since José Mendoza had been out there, making his way through the minefield of dating. For that matter, his father didn't even have any experiences to fall back on.

As far as Jorge knew, his mother had been his father's first girlfriend. His *only* girlfriend. And José Mendoza had found that the best way to get along with his wife was to always back her up and agree with her.

What he needed, Jorge thought, was to talk to someone who had walked in his shoes. Was still walking in his shoes.

There was only one person he knew like that.

Taking a breath, Jorge glanced at his watch. Roberto lived in Denver these days. He tried to remember if there was a time difference between Red Rock and Denver and couldn't. But at most, it was only an hour, he reasoned. That still didn't make it too late to call his older brother.

Roberto, as he recalled, never went to bed before midnight. At least, he hadn't when he lived in Red Rock. Pausing to remember all the numbers in their proper order, Jorge pressed the keypad accordingly.

The phone rang several times and then the answering machine picked up.

Jorge swore under his breath.

Tempted to hang up, he decided to wait out the machine on the off chance that Roberto was either screening his calls or unable to get to the phone before it launched the answering machine.

When the "beep" finally went off, Jorge began to talk.

"Roberto, are you there? It's me, Jorge, and I'd really like to talk to you." He paused for a second, waiting, but nothing happened. No one picked up. Tamping down his irritation, he said, "Okay, well, when you get this, you know where to reach me. I—"

There was a noise on the other end and, for a moment, Jorge thought that the machine was cutting him off. But then he heard his brother's deep voice come on the line. "Jorge? What's wrong? Did something happen to Mom? To Pop?"

"Nothing happened to anyone," Jorge was quick to assure him.

He heard his brother mutter something unintelligible under his breath. Clearing his throat, Roberto asked, "Then why the hell are you calling so late? Date go sour on you?"

Jorge heard a small, amused sound follow the question. At least Roberto hadn't lost his sense of humor, he thought.

"No, it didn't turn 'sour' on me. But that *is* why I'm calling."

There was a prolonged pause on the other end of the line. "It's been a while since I've seen you, Jorge. Maybe that's why I'm not following this. What the hell are you talking about?"

Jorge sighed. "Okay, let me start over again."

"Go for it," his brother encouraged magnanimously.

Jorge took a breath before beginning. "There's this woman—"

He heard Roberto chuckle to himself. "There's always a woman."

Irritation got the better of Jorge. "You want to hear this or not?"

"Sure, I'm not going anywhere—except maybe back to bed," he said the last word pointedly. "Go ahead."

His brother was going to bed early these days? Jorge refrained from asking. Instead, he leaped to the center of his problem.

"She's different."

The word covered a broad spectrum of things and Jorge wasn't being very specific or informative. "Different how?" Roberto wanted to know.

"I don't know." That was part of the problem. He

couldn't quite put his finger on what exactly made Jane stand out for him, but he gave it a shot. "For one thing, she's not a knockout. But she is pretty," Jorge added quickly.

"Okay." Roberto had never known his brother to go out with a woman who wasn't. "I take it that you've slept with her."

Now that he thought about it, Jorge realized that any woman he'd taken an interest in, he'd slept with. Until Jane.

"No."

"No," Roberto repeated incredulously, certain he hadn't heard right.

"No," Jorge echoed, a touch of annoyance entering his voice.

There was another long pause on the other end of the line before Roberto finally said, "I see."

"See what?" Jorge demanded. Since when did Roberto talk in code? "Because I don't."

Rather than answer, Roberto had his younger brother backtrack in his narrative. "Why haven't you slept with her?"

"Because she's not the type for a one-night stand," Jorge told him. He didn't know if that irritated him or made him proud—and the ambivalence was driving him crazy. "She teaches kids how to read, Roberto. She dresses up like one of the characters in the books she reads and goes to the hospital to entertain sick kids."

"Uh-huh." He made it sound like a doctor analyzing symptoms.

Jorge caught himself bristling at the sound. "What's that supposed to mean?"

Rather than explain any further, or even deal with his brother's newfound dilemma, Roberto sighed. There was almost a hopelessness about the sound.

"Look, Jorge, I'd like to help you out here, I really would. I'd like to be able to say something insightful to you to make everything fall into place, but the truth of it is, I'm probably the *last* person you should come to asking for any kind of romantic advice."

He hadn't expected to hear anything like that from Roberto. As far back as he could remember, his brother, who'd once worked in construction and was now heavily into real estate, still managing to maintain a fantastic physique, had always charmed the ladies. There'd never been a problem when it came to Roberto's love life, unless, maybe, that it had involved too many ladies at the same time.

"Since when?" Jorge wanted to know.

"Since I had a reality check."

It was obvious to Jorge that whatever the problem had been—or was—Roberto was not about to disclose it. Jorge switched subjects for a moment. "Why don't you move back home, Roberto? Mom and Pop miss you. So do the rest of us."

"Yeah, well maybe someday," Roberto said evasively, giving him no more of an answer than he had the last time he'd asked his brother to move back to Red Rock. "Look, I really have to go, Jorge. Good luck with this woman—" he paused for a second "what did you say her name was?"

"I didn't. It's Jane," Jorge told him. "Jane Gilliam."

"Well, good luck with this Jane." Roberto sounded as if he was about to hang up, then apparently had a change of heart because he stopped to add, "And welcome to the club."

There was a "click" on the other end of the line. Roberto had hung up before he could ask him exactly what he'd meant by *that*.

Chapter Eleven

"More flowers?"

It was half a question, half an announcement as Sally walked into the lounge several afternoons later. Her hands were wrapped around an ice-blue vase that was stuffed to overflowing with a dozen and a half plump pink roses that had just been delivered to ReadingWorks' door.

Setting down the vase on the table, she gave Jane a long, envious look.

"Just what is it that's going on between the two of you?" she asked. The slight smirk on her lips testified that she thought she already knew the answer to that question.

"And does he have any brothers?" Cecilia wanted

to know, wistfully skimming her fingertips over one of the roses.

As she did so, the card that had been tucked in between the long-stemmed roses came loose. It fell to the table like an open invitation.

Seeing it there, Jane fairly sprinted across the room. She managed to get to the small envelope before either Sally or Cecilia had a chance to pick it up and read what was written inside.

"Yes, he does, I think," Jane told Cecilia. "An older brother living in Denver."

"That's right—Roberto," Cecilia remembered now that Jane mentioned it. "I always wondered why he flew the coop."

Sally paused, trying to remember. "It had something to do with Francine Fortune, didn't it?"

Jane shook her head. She was uncomfortable discussing things she felt that Jorge would rather keep private. "I have no idea. I don't pump Jorge for information."

Harriet walked into the lounge, carrying a new shipment of books meant for school libraries in the poorer sections of Red Rock, a wicked grin gracing her full mouth. She put the box of books down on the floor. "What do you pump Jorge for?"

Jane turned a bright shade of scarlet almost instantly. She could feel the color, rising up her throat, traveling along her cheeks.

"Nothing," she answered tersely as she ripped the envelope open. Focused on reading the note inside, she didn't realize that Sally was right behind her. The older woman rose up on her toes in order to be able to read over her shoulder.

These blushing pink roses reminded me of you, Jane read. *Looking forward to this Friday. Love, Jorge.*

She had less than a second to savor the words.

"So, what does he do to make you blush?" Sally wanted to know, a huge grin accompanying the question.

Startled, Jane swung around, pressing the note to her breast to keep anyone else from reading it.

"He probably just grins at her," Harriet speculated. "That seems to be enough to get her going."

Cecilia draped her arm around Jane's shoulder and gave her a quick squeeze. "Don't mind them, honey. Right now, you're probably the only one in the group who's getting any and they're all just trying to live vicariously."

Jane pulled away, offended at the implication and at the cavalier way the other woman regarded lovemaking. In her eyes lovemaking was supposed to be something special, not a way to just while away the time.

"I'm not 'getting any,'" Jane insisted. "It's not like that."

Harriet looked at her as if she'd just announced to the world at large that she had landed on Mars. "Let me get this straight. You and Jorge aren't sleeping together?"

Jane shook her head adamantly. "No." The single word practically shot out of her mouth.

Harriet's dark eyebrows drew together. "And he's sending you flowers."

"Obviously," Sally answered before Jane could say anything.

Her eyebrows returned to their rightful positions as the smile on Harriet's face widened. "And he's 'looking forward' to Friday night." She repeated the phrase as if there were a conclusion to be drawn from the simple wording.

Jane definitely didn't care for the barely veiled implication.

"We're going to see a play," she told the other women defensively. "And then we're going out to dinner."

"Followed soon after by 'dessert,'" Harriet interjected.

Cecilia was the oldest and, consequently, the most like a den mother. "Leave her alone," she told the other two women. "Whatever she's doing she's doing it right." She turned to Jane. "You just enjoy yourself, kid. And don't do anything you don't want to do," she underscored deliberately.

Harriet looked stunned. "How could she not want to go to bed with Jorge Mendoza?" she wanted to know. "How could *any* woman not want to go to bed with Jorge Mendoza?"

"Your three o'clock student is here, Jane," Sally announced suddenly, seeing the gangly, dark-haired preteen and his mother walking up to the door through the side window.

Jane offered up silent thanks as she hurried off to

the classroom without another word. It was a relief to get back to what she felt she did best. Teaching children how to read.

She didn't have to look at the calendar to know down to the second how long she and Jorge had been seeing each other. She and Jorge had been seeing one another now for almost three weeks. Three weeks of expecting the phone not to ring even as she prayed it would. Three weeks of trying to brace herself for the inevitable onslaught of loneliness while simultaneously making bargains with God for just one more date. Just one more hour with him.

So far, God was saying yes and the phone was ringing at regular intervals.

As Jorge pulled his car into the last available space in guest parking, Jane thought of the comments the women at ReadingWorks had made the other day when the roses had arrived. She knew they were a little envious of her, although she didn't think they were actually jealous. They were too nice for that.

She also doubted that they believed her when she said she wasn't sleeping with Jorge.

But she wasn't.

He had been nothing but a perfect gentleman each and every time they went out. Not once had he even tried to push the issue of sex, silently or otherwise.

Maybe, she thought as they walked up to her door, he didn't really want to. Maybe he thought of her as a respite. A rest period in between his trysts.

For all she knew, he could be seeing someone else even now. He hadn't said anything about only seeing her and no one else. Hadn't even asked her if she wanted to date him exclusively or be free to go out with someone else.

Right, she thought, as if there were actually any danger of that happening. She wasn't exactly beating men away from her doorstep with a stick—or even a toothpick. She never had.

When they came to her door, Jorge leaned one hand just above her head, creating a very intimate alcove for just the two of them.

"You look pretty tonight," he told her. The smile on his lips was golden. It worked its way straight to her insides, turning everything upside down. As usual. "I don't think I told you that earlier."

Every word he'd said to her was forever pressed between the pages of her mind. "No," she whispered. "You didn't."

"Well, you do," he affirmed.

Crooking his finger, Jorge placed it beneath her chin, raising it up just a fraction. His lips touched hers almost in slow motion, as if he were a high school freshman seeking his first kiss instead of the experienced lover everyone knew he was.

Jane instantly felt herself melting, her heart hammering so hard, she was certain he had to feel it pounding against his chest. No doubt about it, whether he kissed her quickly or slowly, deeply or lightly, the man's lips evoked the same kind of reaction from her. Within moments of contact, Jane could feel her inner core heating up, could feel desire and passion galloping through her.

The kiss deepened, taking her to places she'd longed to explore—with Jorge. Each time, he took her a little further. This time was no exception.

And then, just as abruptly, just when she thought that this time, Jorge was going to go further than he had before, perhaps sweep her into his arms, carry her into her apartment and finally make love with her, it all stopped.

Drawing his head back, Jorge fought to regain his grasp on control.

It wasn't easy.

This time, despite all his silent promises to himself, despite his pride in always being able to pull away whenever he decided to, he'd almost gone over the edge. And he knew it.

And it scared the hell out of him.

Scared him because she'd tempted him more than any other woman he'd ever been with. Made him want her with a fierceness that he was completely unaccustomed to. A fierceness that almost wrenched control out of his hands. He didn't like that. A man who lost control could do things he wasn't proud of.

"I'd better go," he told her in a whisper, his breath feathered along her face.

Disappointment sprang up instantly, riding roughshod over her. The words came out before she could stop them. "Why don't you want me?"

He stared at her, not sure he'd heard correctly. "What?"

"Why don't you want me?" she repeated. "The women I work with, your cousin, Isabella, *everyone*," she emphasized, "says that you're a fiery Latin lover." She didn't know where she was getting the courage to continue, but she pushed on. "That no woman is safe with you—that no woman *wants* to be safe with you…"

And then, for a second, her courage flagged along with her self-esteem and her voice trailed off. It took her more than a moment to grab on to a second surge of courage. "But you don't want me."

He laughed softly to himself, shaking his head. Oh God, was she ever wrong.

Ever so tenderly, he lightly skimmed his fingertips through her hair, pushing back the curls that had fallen into her face. He looked into it for a long moment.

"Is that what you think?"

Fidgeting inside, Jane wanted to look away. She forced herself to maintain eye contact. She was tired of being so mousy, so low-key.

"It's hard not to," she told him. "I mean, you kiss me and make my knees weak and just when I think that you're going to press your advantage, you don't. You back off instead."

"Advantage," he repeated the word she'd used. She'd made his point for him—even though it was hard to stand by it when she looked so damn wide-eyed and tempting. "That's the key word. I don't want to take advantage of you, Jane."

Jane heard only what she thought she heard. Proof. "Then I was right." It was hard to keep the hurt tears back, but she managed. "You *don't* want to make love with me."

She couldn't believe she was actually saying that to him, but just this once, she had to make her feelings known. He'd worked her up to the point that she thought she was going to explode—and then he'd just backed away, leaving her to deal with this bubbling cauldron of frustration and desire.

"No, I don't want to take advantage of you," he repeated. "There's a difference."

Unspoken words weighed heavily on his conscience. Each time he saw her, they grew a little heavier. He'd never intended to tell her this, had never wanted her to find out. Especially once he'd gotten to know her. He was ashamed to admit that he'd been a party to something so juvenile. But Jane deserved the truth, he thought, even if it was going to make her hate him.

Heaven knew he couldn't blame her if she did, but he fervently hoped that somehow, she could find it in her heart to forgive him.

She deserved the truth, he thought again, but she didn't deserve to be hurt.

It was a hell of a dilemma he found himself in. Damned if he did and damned if he didn't. And what was worse, he would be hurting someone sweet and innocent who shouldn't be made to feel as if she were nothing more than a pawn.

God, he wished he'd never started this. But then, if he hadn't, he might never have even noticed her. And that would have been a terrible shame.

He paused for a moment, then decided that this confession was best made in private, away from any passing strangers.

"Can we go inside?" he asked.

"All right." Turned away from him, she took out her house keys. Jane tried not to notice that her hand was shaking as she unlocked the front door.

She turned on the light switch by the door. For some reason, the light seemed to accent the darkness. Nerves tap-danced through her.

She shouldn't have pressed the issue, she upbraided herself.

Jorge slowly closed the door behind them. The sound of the lock slipping into its groove seemed louder than it usually did as it ricocheted around the quiet apartment.

Damn, this was hard, he thought. But it had to be done, had to be said. Had to be gotten out into the open and out of the way.

He took a breath, then said, "I haven't been completely honest with you."

Here it came. "You're seeing someone else," she guessed.

Unexpected, the question took him aback. "No."

Was he lying? Was that why he'd hesitated? No, he wasn't like that. She couldn't make herself believe that he could look her in the eyes and lie.

She took another guess. "You're seeing me because you're resting up in between women. Taking a break from being a lover."

It was hard for him not to laugh out loud at that

one. The corners of his mouth curved, though, betraying his amusement. "No."

Then she had no clue where he was going with this. "Okay, I'm out of guesses."

That was because her mind didn't stoop to this level, he thought. She didn't think in terms this low.

Damn, he wished he'd never talked to Ricky Jamison that night. This had all started out innocently enough, as an object lesson. All he'd initially wanted to do was give the boy some confidence. It had never been his intention to hurt anyone.

Nor had it *ever* been his intention to fall for the woman Ricky had selected.

He needed to couch this in the best possible terms he knew how. "I want you to know that I wouldn't hurt you for the world."

Jane felt herself bracing for a blow. She didn't like the way that sounded, but she was the one who had asked, who had pressed him to tell her why he didn't want to make love with her. Whatever came now was on her head, not his. "But?"

The word shimmered between them, a gunshot waiting to go off.

He ordinarily didn't have any trouble framing his thoughts. But right now, it felt as if his mouth were filled with shards of glass. "Do you remember New Year's Eve?"

That was an odd question, she thought. "I'm twenty-five years old," she reminded him. "Senility isn't supposed to set in for at least another forty, fifty years or so." It was her turn to smile, amused. "Yes, I remember New Year's Eve."

"There were a lot of people at the party that night—" He was stalling and he knew it. Jorge forced himself to get to the point. "Including Ricky Jamison. Emmett's adopted son," he added in case the name was unfamiliar to her.

She didn't know the son, but she knew the father. And his wife. "Emmett Jamison," she repeated. "The man who threw the party, right."

Each word felt like a heavy marble in his mouth. "Anyway, Ricky was feeling pretty down on himself that night and he asked me what he could do to get a girl to pay attention to him. He said he'd been watching me and I made it seem easy," Jorge added with a careless shrug, wanting to make sure she understood that he didn't regard that as a compliment. "Ricky said he had no idea how to even talk to a girl." Jorge paused, taking a breath. "I told him that it was simple." Did that sound as pompous as he thought it did? "All he had to do was just pay attention to whoever he was talking to." He stopped. That wasn't what he'd said—he'd whitewashed it. If he was going to tell her the truth, it had to be the entire truth. "Actually, what I said to him was to make the girl feel like she was the prettiest girl in the room. Ricky wanted to know if that always worked and I said yes.

"He still looked pretty uncertain so I volunteered to prove it to him. I told him to pick someone out and I would show him how it was done." He felt like a total heel, slimier by the moment. Well, he'd come this far, he might as well finish. She could probably guess the rest, but he would confirm it. He took a deep breath. "That someone was you."

Jane said nothing. Instead, she looked at Jorge for a long moment, surprised that he would admit this.

Was it guilt that had him confessing?

Or could it be that Jorge actually had feelings for her?

More than likely, he was probably just telling her that the game was over and that he didn't want to continue with it anymore.

The silence felt as if it were dragging on and on. Each second killing him.

"Say something," he implored. Jorge knew he deserved a tongue-lashing. Why wasn't she yelling at him? Calling him a lowlife? Why was she just looking at him like that? "Say *anything*."

And then Jane said the one thing he never expected.

"I know."

Chapter Twelve

"You know?"

Jorge stared at Jane, certain he had misunderstood.

"Yes," she told him quietly, her subdued tone not giving him any kind of a clue as to her emotions. "You had a bet."

Jorge continued studying her face, looking for some kind of sign he could recognize, some feeling that he could identify.

"When?" he wanted to know. "When did you find out?" And then the answer suddenly came to him. Things began to fall into place. "When I went to get your coat," Jorge realized. "That was why you disappeared, wasn't it?"

She would have thought a man as smart as Jorge would have figured that out a long time ago. But then, he'd never been on her side of the fence, never dealt with humiliation.

"Yes, that was why. I didn't want to be the butt of a joke. Even yours."

Dear God, she made it sound almost like an apology when *he* should be the one apologizing. The one trying to make things up to her. Regret and shame drenched him.

He tried to make sense of the pieces before him. "Then why did you go out with me?" he asked. Heaven knew he wouldn't have if the tables had been turned— unless he was out for revenge. But that wasn't Jane. Jane Gilliam didn't have a vengeful bone in her body— he was willing to bet his soul on that. "When I showed up at ReadingWorks with your coat and the picnic basket, why didn't you just tell me where to go?"

Her next words confirmed what he'd been thinking. She shook her head.

"That's not me," Jane told him. "I don't like causing scenes. Besides, everyone there thought that I had hit some kind of romantic lottery." She slipped off her coat and draped it on the back of the recliner near her.

"And," she went on, "if you must know, I was just kind of curious how far you'd take this bet. Besides, I have to admit that you're so very good looking, so very charming, it's hard to think of you as an evil, self-centered jerk I should have just sent on his way."

"I'm not a jerk," he protested. "I'm not evil," he insisted. "But what you said about self-centered…

maybe you're right. Maybe I don't see beyond my personal space. Or, at least, I didn't."

He slipped his arms around her, drawing her in a little closer. Relieved that she didn't pull pack. He would have deserved it if she had, but he was glad she didn't.

"It took you to make me realize that. To broaden my way of looking at things." Unlike some of the lines he'd fed other women in the past, this time he meant every word he was saying.

A smile slowly, shyly, stole over her lips. "You don't have to say all that," she told him. "You've already got me."

It surprised Jorge that her words actually excited him, stirred him in a way he hadn't been stirred in a very long time.

But before he could go forward, there were still loose ends to tie up, air to clear.

"I'm not saying it to 'get' you, Jane. I'm saying it because it's true. I honestly don't know what it is about you, whether it's your innate goodness or because you always seem to look for the best in people, but you make me want to be the best person I possibly can. For you."

He thought she'd be pleased. Instead, she shook her head. "You should be the best person you possibly can be for *you*."

Their eyes met for a long moment. "I don't deserve the best person," he told her, his meaning clear. That in his opinion, *she* was the best person. Far better than he.

She smiled. "Yes, you do." For possibly the first time in her life, she felt in control of a situation. Or at least an equal in it. But she didn't want to be in control. She just wanted to share whatever was about to happen. "Now, are you going to kiss me?" she asked, thrilled at her own boldness. "Or are we going to talk all night?"

He smiled into her eyes, liking this brand-new layer to Jane that he'd uncovered. "We could talk if you wanted to."

Her eyes on his, she slowly moved her head from side to side. "Uh-uh. Maybe later."

Actually, she was really praying for later, really hoping that once this moment blossomed and played itself out, that Jorge would still want to stay here, still want to be with her and just lay beside her. At least for a little while.

His mouth curved invitingly, exciting her. "Whatever you want."

The next moment, his lips were on hers as he tugged at her pullover, loosening it and then dragging it away from her body. For a split second, his lips left hers, only to recapture them hungrily a moment later as her pullover cascaded onto the rug at her feet.

Jane shivered against him, even though she was sure her body temperature had gone up by several degrees, erupting in flames as his hands stroked her arms, her shoulders, her bare sides.

Hungers and sensations she was entirely unfamiliar with went racing through her.

She was aware of everything, yet all seemed to be

happening inside a blazing haze. One that would consume her at any moment.

Strong, gentle, urgent fingers were unzipping her skirt, coaxing it down her hips. Goose bumps materialized on her arms from the intimate contact. Her breath was coming in smaller and smaller snatches as excitement all but constricted her lungs.

Jane struggled to concentrate, to do something beyond merely being a vessel that was swiftly being filled with all these delicious feelings as Jorge freed her from her clothing one article at a time.

She wanted to *do* something, to make him feel the kind of anticipation that she was experiencing. She didn't want to disappoint him.

Desire pulsed within her, coloring everything in hues of red.

Only vaguely was she aware of unbuttoning Jorge's shirt, of pushing the dark blue material off his shoulders. She was acutely aware of her skin seeking the warmth of his.

It was almost as if she were on automatic pilot, flying blindly into territory where she had never been before, hadn't even known of before, much less had a knowledge of its terrain.

All she knew was that she didn't want this to stop.

When she felt his lips move to the hollow of her throat, she thought she would just implode right then and there.

Instincts took over, instincts she hadn't even suspected she had. Instincts that drove her to do things she hadn't even *thought* about doing.

Jane mimicked Jorge's earlier movements, stripping off his clothing, letting her eager mouth roam over his throat, forging a passage along his bare, muscular chest. She felt him shiver. Empowered, her lips, teeth and tongue passed over his hard, taut skin.

She thought she heard him catch his breath and the very sound sent ripples of wild excitement through her. It gave her the courage to continue on her journey, the courage to *hang* on even while a part of her just wanted to fall back and absorb all that he had to offer. All that he was doing to her.

Jane wasn't certain just how it happened, but somewhere along the line, they wound up near the piles of shed clothing, on the floor.

Their mouths sealed to one another, they rolled into one another, switching positions as the momentum overtook one of them or the other, fueled by eagerness to be submerged in as many sensations, as many passions as humanly possible.

He'd been in the presence of expert lovers before, women who knew just what to do to work a man into a frenzy, bringing him to his knees. Knew how to make him want the final act, the climax, more than life itself.

But there was something more at work here. Something that he couldn't begin to reconcile or work into his vast knowledge of what made people, what made *women* tick. When it came to Jane, along with what he could testify was an expertise, a finesse that was hard won and long in formation, he could have sworn there was an innocence at its core.

How was that possible?

How could she be a consummate lover and yet an eager novice at the same time?

Who was this woman really? More important, he thought, how could he make her want to remain with him?

Jorge heard her whimper in sheer ecstasy as he skimmed his lips over her abdomen. Watched in fascination as the muscles there quivered in response, even as she raised her hips to him in an open invitation.

Slowly moving his heated body over hers, watching desire bloom like twin dark flowers in her eyes, Jorge gently kneed her legs apart.

Beginning to enter, he stopped, startled as resistance met him. Not hers, but an actual physical barrier.

That could only be for one reason.

Stopping, Jorge raised himself up on his elbows, pivoting over her body as he looked at her in confusion. "Jane?"

She made no response. He wasn't even sure if she'd heard him. Instead, she thrust her hips up against his in a hard, swift movement that he could no more resist than he could will himself to stop breathing.

Her mouth quickly sealed itself to his as a cry of pain was about to escape. The sound was muffled against his lips.

Jorge was aware of rigid tension shooting through her body for an instant before it relaxed once more.

The next moment, she began to move against him in a timeworn rhythm.

Unable to resist, to tamp down his own needs and back away, Jorge got caught up in the rhythm. He took the lead, his hips sealed to hers the same way his mouth was.

And the tempo of the dance they engaged in grew quicker and quicker until he found that they were racing toward that final moment, that final sensation that would make them both feel, just for the tiniest split second, immortal.

He felt her tense again, but this time it was in a good way. She'd tensed and held on to him with both hands digging into his shoulders. It was as if she were desperately trying to hold on to the moment, on to the godlike sensation that was completely covered with extreme happiness.

But even as she held on, it began to break apart, to fade away into the mists, leaving behind two spent, heated bodies in its wake.

He felt her breathing grow steadier, felt her relaxing in almost a dreamlike state.

Rising up on his elbows, Jorge withdrew from her. Then, in a fluid motion, rather than just get up and walk away, he laid down next to her. Pressing a kiss to her forehead, he tucked one arm around her as he held her to him.

Confusion held his conscience prisoner.

How did he even broach this?

He'd never been in this position before. Virginity had only been involved once in all his liaisons, and it had been *his* virginity that had been lost, not that of the woman he had made love with.

"Why didn't you tell me?" he finally asked.

Here it came, she thought. The moment she'd been dreading. It had been that obvious to him.

"Tell you what?" she murmured.

Her voice sounded different than usual. Was that wariness he heard? Defensiveness?

He couldn't tell.

Maybe he was mistaken. Maybe she wasn't a virgin. Maybe she was just built very, very small.

No, he knew what he knew and this time, he had to take responsibility for what he'd done from the start rather than just hope that the subject would never come up.

"Why didn't you tell me that you were a virgin?" Jorge wanted to know, enunciating each word slowly, carefully.

She fought back the embarrassment, the suddenly feeling of vulnerability. "You mean you missed it on my business card? Jane Gilliam," she recited, "BA, MA, and, oh yes, PV."

"PV?" What the hell was PV? He'd never come across that degree.

"Professional Virgin," she elaborated. "Possibly the last one over the age of twenty in this part of Texas."

He hadn't meant to embarrass her. If anything, he was the one who was embarrassed. Embarrassed by his cavalier treatment of her when she should have had a better introduction to this world.

"Jane—"

"If I told you I was a virgin, would you have made love with me?" It was almost an accusation rather than a question.

He had to be honest with her. "No."

His answer stung, shooting an arrow straight into her heart. But she hadn't expected anything else. She'd just hoped...

"Well, there you have it." She stared up at the ceiling rather than look at him. She couldn't bear to see the disappointment in his eyes—or worse. "That's why I didn't tell you. Because I knew you didn't want to waste your time and considerable talents making love with a woman who couldn't return the favor."

Because she was staring at the ceiling, he took her chin in his hand and turned her head, forcing her to look at him.

"I wouldn't have made love with you—no matter how much I wanted to—because a woman's first time is supposed to be special."

That temporarily stopped her in her tracks. Jane looked at him for a long moment, trying to decide if it was just an excuse he was hiding behind, or if he could actually mean what he was saying. He was Jorge Mendoza. That alone made it special.

"What makes you think it wasn't?" she asked incredulously. "That was why I chose you. I wanted you to be the first."

And the last, but I can't tell you that. You'll run out the door, naked, to get away from me.

"You still should have told me," he insisted.

No, she shouldn't have. "Then you wouldn't have been the first," she countered.

Yes, God help him, he would have. He wouldn't have been able to get up and walk away, not after they'd gone that far. He wasn't made of iron, only flesh. "I would have gone slower."

A sad smile crept over her lips. "Any slower and I would have caught fire," she told him. "Don't worry. I know that this doesn't mean anything to you. I'm not about to chain you to my bed—if we were in bed," she amended. "I just wanted—"

"Will you be quiet?" he told her.

But she needed to get this out. This could be the last time she'd ever see him. "I—"

"Obviously not," he said more to himself than to her. "Okay, only one way I know how to handle this," he told her.

And the next minute, moved in a way he'd never been before, wanting Jane all over again when by all rights, he should have been spent and all but asleep, he gathered her to him again and brought his mouth down on hers.

Startled, the moment their lips parted, she asked breathlessly, "What are you doing?"

She watched as an amused smile danced on his very tempting lips.

"If you have to ask, then I guess I didn't do it right the first time," he said against her lips.

And then there was no space for any further conversation. He was too busy showing her.

Chapter Thirteen

What the hell had he been thinking?

The question throbbed over and over in Jorge's head like a relentless tattoo five seconds after he had woken up the next morning.

He was lying beside Jane, who mercifully, appeared to be still asleep.

Their night of lovemaking, which had moved, in a flurry of clothing and passions, from the living room through the tiny hall until it had finally ended up here in her bedroom—in her bed, vividly came back to him. In living color.

Guilt attacked at the same time, coming at him from all sides, aided and abetted by fear. Fear of consequences, fear of what this all ultimately meant.

Jane wasn't the type of woman a man had a one-night stand with or even a brief affair. She might have protested last night that she didn't expect what was happening between them to mean anything to him, but he knew that in her heart, she was hoping that it did.

And it did, which was what scared him.

He wasn't husband material. He wasn't even boy-friend material, Jorge thought. No matter how good his intentions might be, he knew himself. Knew that before long, another woman would attract his attention, catch his fancy and he'd be off, leaving Jane behind and breaking her heart.

Or, worse, he'd remain with her and grow to resent the shackles that bound him.

Why the hell had he slept with her? He couldn't even blame this on anything he had to drink because he hadn't had anything to drink. If he'd been intoxicated last night at all, it was with the moment—and her.

She was still sleeping. He needed to go. Now, before there was a need for dialogue.

Very slowly, moving a fraction of an inch at a time, Jorge drew away from Jane until he was finally out of the bed.

His clothes, Jorge recalled, were still in the living room. That left him to make his way to the living room stark naked. He couldn't take the sheet off the bed. Half of it was on her side. He didn't want to risk waking her up for the sake of modesty.

When the hell had he started to care about that? he

wondered suddenly. It felt like everything about him, about the way he conducted his life, was going through some kind of upheaval. He couldn't deal with this.

With stealth movements, Jorge began to slowly tiptoe toward the door. He'd only made it halfway when he heard rustling behind him.

Jane.

Was she just turning in her sleep, or was she awake? Summoning courage, he forced himself to turn around to look at her.

Their eyes met.

And the look in hers told him that he didn't have to bother coming up with excuses. She knew what he was doing. Fleeing without saying goodbye.

But he had to say something, didn't he? Besides, the excuse was actually true, it just wasn't the main reason he was going.

"I have a meeting," he told her.

God, did that sound as lame to her as it did to him? He tried to remember the last time he'd actually felt this awkward and couldn't. What had this woman with the deep, soulful eyes done to him?

"Okay." Her response sounded almost cheerful.

Sitting up, she wrapped the sheet around herself like a toga before she swung her legs off the bed and onto the floor.

This was just what he *hadn't* wanted. A prolonged goodbye. "You really don't have to get up," Jorge told her.

"I was going to make you coffee," she informed

him with a smile. Then, as if reading what he was thinking, she emphasized, "Not breakfast, just coffee." As if accepting anything to eat would somehow bind him to her, but coffee was universally acceptable. "Besides," she went on, "I'd like some coffee, too."

"Oh, all right." The words came out incredibly stilted.

Jorge sounded almost nervous, she thought. Did he expect her to jump him because he possessed the most perfect male body ever created? She did her best to concentrate on his face, but just being in the presence of his nakedness was enough to raise her body temperature by several degrees. She did what she could to seem unaffected.

"Why don't you get dressed and I'll work on the coffee," she suggested nonchalantly. Oscars, she thought, were given for lesser performances.

As she walked passed him, her eyes deliberately focused on the doorway, she heard him call out her name. "Jane—"

Jane glanced over her shoulder, careful to make only eye contact. "No food," she assured him with a smile, "Just coffee to wake you up for the meeting."

"Right."

She walked to the kitchen as he quickly went to the living room.

You would have thought she was the experienced one and he was the newly deflowered virgin, Jorge thought, disgusted with his reaction, with his sudden inability to sound aloof, as he hurried into his clothes. She was handling this with a lot more grace than he was.

Dressed, he walked into the kitchen, brought there more by a sense of contrition than by the deep, enticing smell of brewing coffee. Jane was still wearing the sheet, artfully tucked around her to allow for movement.

He had to admit, as eager as he was to be on his way and put what he viewed as a big mistake behind him, the thought of reaching out and unraveling the sheet did captivate him for a second.

No. He wasn't going to get entrenched any further. He shouldn't have slept with her—he wasn't going to compound it by doing it again. He had to leave, quickly, while leaving was still an option.

But he couldn't leave without saying something, now that she was awake. That would be the coward's way and he had never been a coward. He wasn't about to become one. "About last night, Heidi," he began, trying to deflect some of the seriousness by calling her the nickname he'd previously given her.

Jane stiffened. She'd really hoped that she would have been able to cling to her fantasy a little longer. More time to pretend that life could actually arrange itself for her benefit just this once. But she didn't want to ruin the memory of what she did have by having him stumble through some kind of awkward apology or, equally bad, an excuse. That would only taint everything.

"Last night was last night," she said as she poured out two inky cups of coffee. Turning, she placed one on the counter before him and then took hold of the other with both hands. "And today is today," she added with a smile that clearly absolved him of any and all sins he thought he'd committed.

The flood of relief he felt was brief, nudged quickly aside by a sense of confusion. She was acting as if last night hadn't meant anything to her.

"That's it?" he asked, bewildered.

"That's it," she confirmed. "Why?" A small, knowing smile curved her mouth. "Isn't that the way you usually view these encounters?"

Actually, it was. It was his vague justification for moving on, for giving in to the restless wanderlust that came over him periodically, every time he saw a beautiful face or an inviting body. And there was *always* a beautiful face or an inviting body within easy reach.

But admitting it seemed almost sordid. Still, he couldn't very well deny it, could he?

"Yes."

She studied him for a moment, as if trying to formulate a response. "Then why do you look so surprised?"

"Well, I thought that you— That we—" He couldn't find the right words to finish the sentence.

Jane found them for him. "You didn't think it would be this easy?" she guessed. "Did you think I was going to wrap myself around your leg and hold on for dear life? Ask you what you wanted to name the children when they started coming along?" She paused to take a sip of her coffee while he stared at her, for once in his life completely speechless. "I might not be all that experienced, Jorge," she went on, secretly congratulating herself on how calm she sounded. "But I'm not stupid. The prince does not forsake his kingdom for a scullery maid. For Cinderella, maybe, but definitely not for the scullery maid."

That *really* took him by surprise. "Is that how you see yourself?"

"Symbolically," Jane elaborated. She was still smiling complacently at him, as if none of this left a scar or cut deep. "I have no regrets, Jorge. If I'd said no, you would have backed off. I know you would. I didn't want to say no. I knew exactly what I was doing last night—" And then she amended, "Well, most of the time. A few times I was a little out of my head." The smile on her lips filtered into her eyes as well. "But that's just because you do what you do so well."

His guilt increased a thousandfold because she was being so incredibly understanding. He would have done better if she'd ranted at him, called him names. He felt both off the hook and like a consummate heel for feeling that way.

"Jane, I don't—"

She glanced at the clock on the wall. "Didn't you say you have a meeting to go to?" she reminded him, not letting him finish again.

He did. And if it actually wasn't so important, he might have opted to remain.

But it was better this way, he told himself. Jane was giving him a way out, letting him take his leave gracefully and go out the door. He was the one who was spoiling it.

This was just the kind of exit he appreciated.

Putting his cup down on the counter, Jorge paused to brush a quick kiss against her cheek.

"You really are one of a kind, you know that?" he told her quietly.

Her response was glib. "I'll be sure to have that added to my business card, now that I have to have the PV removed." She was smiling as she said it.

That was the way he remembered her as he made his way out the door. Smiling.

That was the way she wanted him to remember her. And he'd left not a moment too soon.

Jane wasn't sure how much longer she could have kept up the charade, how much longer she could have had her lips continue to form that mindless smile that was all but glued in place.

Not easy smiling like that when your heart was shattering into a thousand pieces right there in your chest, she thought.

Her shoulders sagged as she abandoned her half-finished coffee. Wrapping the bottom of the sheet around her arm to keep from tripping on it, she went to the living room and began to pick up her discarded clothing one piece at a time.

And as she did so, last night vividly returned to her, replaying itself in her head. If she closed her eyes, she could even feel Jorge's hands on her, gently gliding along her flesh. Could smell the scent of his skin as he held her close to him.

No matter what she'd said to Jorge just now, or pretended that she believed for his sake, she knew she was in love with him. Had fallen in love from the moment he first walked up to her.

But that was for her to deal with, not him. He could never know, could never even suspect, what it was she felt for him.

And, truth be told, she'd gotten more out of their brief time together than she'd ever hoped for. Jane nursed no false image of herself. She knew all her good qualities. Being a bombshell was not among them.

And yet she, the bookish, mousy daughter of a former beauty queen had managed, just for a little while, to be with a man who invaded so many women's dreams. Be with him in every sense of the word.

That was more than most women had, she thought. Certainly more than she had ever thought she would have outside of her daydreams.

Jane stood there for a moment, clutching the clothes she'd worn last night, trying very hard not to give in to the tears that were suddenly forming inside her.

Last night was nothing to cry about. Last night was something to celebrate.

But today, this morning, well, that was something actually worthy of tears, she silently admitted. Because she knew that Jorge wouldn't be back. She had given him his freedom, his exit line, and he had seized them both with relief and gusto.

At least he wouldn't think of her as some clingy, pathetic female.

The thought was supposed to give her solace. But it didn't.

She sank down to the floor where she stood, the sheet pooling haphazardly around her as her tears fell freely.

Sally glanced at the table as she walked into the lounge. It had gotten to be a habit.

"No more flowers?" she asked Jane, who was the only other one there.

More than a week had passed since she'd watched Jorge walk out her front door. A week in which it was everything she could do not to break down while she was out in public.

She wasn't entirely sure how she had managed that. Jane had thrown herself into her job, working out elaborate reading schedules for each child she tutored. After work, she doubled up on the number of hours she volunteered in order to fill her evenings and weekends. She needed to keep busy every single moment. She didn't want to be alone with her thoughts until she could keep them from instantly gravitating toward Jorge.

She was still working on that.

True to her expectations, Jorge hadn't called, hadn't tried to get in touch with her at all.

Why should he?

She'd been his challenge. Now that he'd met it,

been victorious over it, there was no reason to return to the scene of his triumph. After all, there were so many more fish out there in the sea. Prettier, more accomplished fish.

But none of them is ever going to love you the way I do, she told him silently.

As if that mattered to him. He seemed to be doing just fine with those empty-headed beauties who gravitated to him.

"No, no more flowers," Jane replied, trying to keep her voice level and distant. Praying that Sally would be satisfied and just move on.

Obviously, God wasn't answering prayers lately, because all of hers were going by the wayside.

Rather than leave the room, Sally crossed to her and hooked her long arm through hers. The older woman gently drew her over to the sofa.

"Something wrong?" she asked, lowering her voice even though they were the only two people in the lounge.

Jane shook her head, avoiding eye contact. "Nothing's wrong."

Sally tilted her head, trying to get her to look in her direction. "But you two are still dating."

"We were never really dating," Jane told her. She shrugged, doing her best to seem as if none of this bothered her. "Jorge was just…spending time with me."

Sally frowned, trying to understand. "Isn't that what dating is?"

"Not in the real sense of the word," Jane answered sadly.

But she didn't want to get into it, didn't want anyone to know about the bet. It made her seem pathetic and Jorge shallow. She didn't want anyone to think of him that way. She actually understood what he'd been trying to do.

"I'm not his type," was all she said.

Sally looked at her, mystified. "Did he tell you that?"

"No," Jane admitted. "But look at the women he's been seen with."

Sally made a dismissive sound. "None of them hold a candle to you."

Jane laughed sadly, shaking her head. She appreciated what her friend was trying to do. But that still didn't change anything. "Sally, you're sweet, but you're my friend."

Sally sniffed. "I also have 20/20 vision and even better instincts. You are very attractive—when you let yourself be," the woman underscored. "You're also a woman of substance. Any man would be thrilled to have you in his life."

Sally made it sound as if there were men lining up three deep outside her door. "Don't seem to be many of those around," she quipped.

Sally slipped her arm around Jane's shoulders, giving her a comforting squeeze. None of the women who worked here had escaped being dumped by someone they thought was in their life for the long haul. And Jane, the youngest, had had more than her share of heartaches.

"Want to come over tonight, let your hair down? Vent?" Sally suggested.

That was the last thing she wanted to do. Because she knew she'd cry when faced with too much sympathy and she didn't want to cry. Didn't want to talk about it until she could do so calmly.

"Thanks, but I've got to be at the hospital. We're starting a new book. *Peter Pan*."

Sally looked at her in surprise. "You're all finished with *Heidi?*" She'd only started that just before New Year's Eve.

Jane looked away. "Extra readings," she said with a shrug.

Sally sighed, accepting defeat, at least temporarily. "Well, you know where to find me if you change your mind."

Leaving Jane in the room, Sally headed for the door. Jane's students were coming soon and she needed to do a few things before they arrived. Just about to reach for the door, she stepped back quickly as it was swung opened. Harriet burst in, her face contorted with horror. "Have you heard?" she asked.

Sally exchanged glances with Jane. "Heard what?" Sally asked.

"Red is on fire," Harriet declared like a newscaster reporting a breaking story.

Sally's eyes widened with amazement. "The restaurant?"

"No, the color," Harriet retorted with obvious impatience. "Yes, the restaurant."

Jane said nothing. Grabbing her coat, she was already running to the front door.

Chapter Fourteen

Jane didn't even remember getting into her car, or turning the key in the ignition. But somehow, she got out here, on the road, driving faster than she'd ever driven in her life. Fervently praying for all she was worth.

Turning sharply, Jane sucked in her breath as she quickly righted her wheel again. She'd missed colliding with an SUV by inches. With her heart hammering wildly, she saw the driver roll down his window and heard him swear at her. All she could do was wave one hand in a helpless gesture, hoping he'd see her in his mirror and understand that it hadn't been on purpose.

Swallowing, trying to calm herself down, her

heart was still pounding louder than the song that was playing on the radio. With a frustrated twist of her hand, she shut it off. She didn't want music at a time like this, she wanted silence.

Instead, she heard the jarring peal of sirens.

Fire trucks.

Fire, she thought hopelessly. There was a fire. And from the smoke she saw rising in the air, even at this distance, she knew in her heart that it had to be coming from Red.

An icy hand passed over her and she shivered even as she found herself sweating.

Jorge was there.

Inside.

She didn't know how she knew, but she did. She knew with a certainty that went all the way down to her bones. Fear squeezed the very air out of her lungs.

Jane drove faster.

One minute, he was sitting by himself at his table for two, finishing a meal he'd barely tasted. There was nothing to even hint at what was coming. This was Red, the restaurant that was almost like another member of his family. Jorge was more familiar with every nook and cranny of the two-story establishment than he was with the spaces in his own home.

He'd come here searching for a sense of peace that had been eluding him for the last week. Ever since he'd walked away from Jane.

The next minute, just after the first whiff of smoke

seemed to come out of nowhere, suddenly he saw flames racing toward the dining area from the general direction of the kitchen.

It was just after two in the afternoon and most of the regulars who came here for lunch were gone. Only a few stragglers remained, the ones who had no boss eyeing the company clock, no lunch hour that had come to an abrupt end.

A scream pierced the air, followed by the word *Fire,* and suddenly the room was in motion. The few customers who were left jumped to their feet, knocking over chairs as they stampeded for the front door.

Jorge's eyes were riveted toward the kitchen. The noon cook, the busboys, the waitresses—and his father—they were all in there somewhere, lost behind that growing curtain of flames.

He had to get to them.

To his father.

Jorge poured his glass of water onto the napkin he'd just discarded, then fashioned a bandanna out of it, covering his nose and mouth as he hurried toward the belly of the fire.

"Pop!" he yelled, projecting his voice into the flames. "Pop, are you there?"

He thought he heard someone calling back.

Or maybe it was just the groan of the fire. But he couldn't take that chance. He knew that after the lunch crowds abated, his father liked to retreat to his small office behind the kitchen to go over tallies. The older Mendoza hadn't come out to see him yet, so that meant that he was still there. Trapped by the fire.

"Pop!" Jorge yelled again. He crouched low to avail himself of any oxygen in the room.

That was how he wound up stumbling into Juan, one of the part-time busboys who was groping around blindly and heading in the wrong direction.

The fire was growing more intense.

"That way!" Jorge yelled over the roar of the flames. Grabbing Juan's shoulders, he physically turned the thin busboy around because the latter couldn't seem to comprehend what he was saying. Wide, frightened eyes looked up at him. "My father," Jorge shouted at him. "Have you seen my father?"

The light seemed to dawn on Juan. "In his office," the boy blurted out. Juan moved his hand about wildly, not realizing that he was pointing toward the salad bar. The latter had become a casualty of a fallen overhead beam.

"Go!" Jorge ordered. "Go that way!" Again, he pointed toward the front of the restaurant. The double doors were still untouched by flames—but for how much longer?

He pushed the busboy toward the doors, then turned back into the restaurant. Feeling incredibly light-headed, Jorge wove in and out, looking for a path to the office that wasn't completely obstructed by flames. Flames were hungrily devouring everything around him.

The heat was unbearable.

What if this was it? his mind screamed. What if he was meant to die today? Here, in the place where he had practically grown up.

In the place where he had first met Jane.

Jane.

Oh, God, he was going to die and she was going to think he didn't love her. That he didn't want her.

He could have had a life with her, Jorge thought in despair, and he'd thrown it all away. The very reason he was here today was because he was desperately trying to bolster his spirits. Deep down, he'd known that turning his back on making a commitment to Jane was the wrong thing to do, yet he was still trying to talk himself into it.

Not anymore.

He'd gotten turned around, Jorge realized, fighting back a panic. Both in his life and in trying to make his way to the kitchen.

The napkin covering his nose and mouth was dry.

He had to get his father out. And he had to live. He had to survive this so that he could tell Jane he was an idiot.

"Pop!" Jorge yelled again, charging through the kitchen, flames swallowing him.

This was a bad one, Darr Fortune thought as he jumped off the fire truck before it came to a full stop. Quickly, he removed his gear from the vehicle.

Red was being destroyed. Hell of a shame. He'd eaten here himself a number of times.

Hell, he suddenly realized, he'd been here New Year's Eve with his dad and siblings. Who would have ever thought that he'd be back four weeks later, fighting to save it? If there was anything left to save.

Behind him, several of the other firefighters were attaching the hose, preparing to douse the two-story building with a flood of water. With any luck, they'd be able to save some of it. With more luck, it would matter that they did. Sometimes, structures struck by fire were so far beyond repair that knocking them down and beginning over was all that was left to do.

Damn shame, Darr thought again.

As he secured the tank, he was suddenly jostled from the side. Turning, he saw a brown-haired woman run past him. She'd obviously broken through the barricade that had been hastily put up.

The damn fool looked like she was running straight for the burning building!

"Hey, hold it!" Darr yelled after her. "You can't go in there!"

Jane didn't even slow down to look at the fire-fighter. "I have to. He's in there. I know it. I have to find him," she cried.

Suddenly, she felt herself being grabbed around the waist by a powerful arm and lifted off the ground in one swift, seemingly effortless movement. The firefighter swung her around 180 degrees away from the restaurant entrance.

"Lady," Darr said as patiently as he could. "I understand how you feel, I really do, but you can't go in there."

She wasn't going be talked out of it. "I have to. I can't let him die in there." She was struggling not to cry, not to let her imagination go any further than it was right at this moment.

"Him?" Darr asked. According to the person who'd called in the fire, one of the patrons, the few people in the restaurant dining area had fled.

"Jorge," she cried. She tried to move past Darr, but he merely blocked her again. "Jorge Mendoza."

The guy whose father owned the place. Darr was vaguely aware that Jorge Mendoza had some kind of a reputation for being a class-A Romeo. He clearly had to be one hell of a lover if this one was willing to risk burning to death trying to find him.

Trying to be gentle, Darr pushed the woman back to the barricade.

"Saving him is my job," he told her, trying to get her behind the sawhorse. "Let me do it."

Just then, a bedraggled, soot-blackened busboy staggered out through the front door. Coughing madly, he gasped in gulps of air. Unable to stand, he collapsed to his knees.

Darr made his way to the boy. The brown-haired woman darted past him, running to the fallen busboy.

Dropping to her knees beside the gasping Juan, Jane cried, "Is Jorge in there?"

The boy nodded vigorously, still trying to drag in enough air to answer her. "He...pointed...the... way...out...for...me," he finally managed to get out.

That was all she needed. Jane scrambled up to her feet, about to run to the double doors.

Again, Darr stopped her. "Murphy!" he yelled to one of the other firefighters.

About to run to the building, the heavyset man,

who looked as if he'd be more at home on a football field, responded to his name and turned to look at Darr.

"Yeah?"

"Keep an eye on this one before she's burned to a crisp," Darr ordered, physically taking hold of Jane by the shoulders and moving her over to Murphy.

"But you don't understand." She tried to wiggle out of the firefighter's grasp and couldn't. "He's in there. I've got to get to him."

"You won't do him any good dead," Darr told her matter-of-factly, hurrying to the restaurant. "I'll tell him you're waiting," was his parting comment to her.

Double-checking the last of his equipment, the stocky, muscular firefighter charged into the burning inferno.

And it was just that. An inferno.

It was hard to see, hard to move. The interior of the dining room looked like it was one continuous sheet of flame.

To the left of the entrance were the rest rooms. That avenue hadn't been discovered by the roaring fire yet, but it was only a matter of seconds before it was.

Darr pushed open the door closest to him. It led to the men's room. "Anyone in here?" he shouted, his voice made surreal by his mask.

The doors all appeared to be unlocked. A quick scan of the floor told him that the area was unoccupied.

Most likely, any patrons or help this close to the

entrance had bolted the second they'd heard cries of "Fire," he thought.

About to move on to the dining room, Darr decided to give the ladies' room a quick check first. Just in case. He shouldered the door opened and yelled out the same question. He received the same answer. Nothing.

But just as he began to withdraw from the room, Darr saw her. Or rather, he saw her legs, peering out from beneath the last stall.

Hurrying over, he shoved open the door and found a young woman on the floor. It looked as if the smoke had gotten to her.

"Lady, lady wake up," Darr ordered.

Her eyes remained closed. He had no time to try to get her to come around. Kneeling, Darr scooped her up into his powerful arms. His equipment felt as if it weighed a ton as he struggled to get back up to his feet. By contrast, the unconscious blonde felt as if she weighed nothing.

"C'mon," he quipped to the unconscious woman as he hurried out with her in his arms, "this is no place to take a nap."

His voice gave no indication of how grateful he was that he'd decided to check the ladies' room.

Jane was just about to dart under the arm of the distracted firefighter when she saw him.

Them.

Jorge and his father.

The older man, sooty and coughing, was leaning heavily on his son. From where she was standing, they looked like two sides of a pyramid that should, by all rights, collapse but was determined not to.

"Jorge!" she screamed. The next second, she broke into a run and was sprinting across the parking lot. She vaguely heard the firefighter who'd been keeping her away from the restaurant yelling after her, but she was not about to stop. Not until she had assured herself that what she was seeing was no mirage. Not until she'd satisfied herself that Jorge was alive and well, and unhurt.

Jane reached Jorge and his father just as Murphy caught up.

José looked as if he was barely standing.

"Oh, my God, is he all right?" Jane cried, immediately going to the older man's other side to help prop him up.

Murphy took over, moving Jane out of the way and grasping the sagging José about the waist.

"He needs oxygen," Jorge told the firefighter, struggling to talk without coughing. It felt as if his lungs were filled with stifling ash and smoke. He gingerly relinquished his own hold on his father. "Careful," he warned just before a coughing fit finally took over.

"I need a paramedic here!" Murphy called out.

Two ambulances had already arrived, butted up side by side on the extreme left of the parking lot. Two teams of emergency medical technicians came running over even before Murphy called for them. One team took charge of José Mendoza while the other two attendants turned their attention to the woman that Darr Fortune was just now carrying out.

But all Jane could see was Jorge. It was a struggle to keep fear from taking over and rendering her useless.

"Are you all right?" she demanded even as she ran her hands along his arms, his face, his torso. She needed to assure herself that he was whole, that she hadn't just conjured him up out of the flames.

Then, before Jorge could attempt to answer, she kissed him, unable to express her incredible gratitude that he was alive any other way. The next moment she pulled back as if a hot poker had speared her, afraid that she was stealing what little oxygen he'd been able to drag back into his lungs.

He was alive.

She felt like laughing and crying at the same time. "I had to come," she explained, shaking. "As soon as I heard, I knew, I knew you were inside."

Her tears began to fall freely. Jane didn't bother trying to stop them. What was the point? She wasn't trying to maintain a facade or somehow guilt Jorge into reconsidering their nonexistent relationship. She was just relieved that he wasn't a victim of the fire.

"This doesn't mean anything," she said, referring to her tears. "I'm not trying to make you feel guilty or anything, I just— Oh God, you're all right. You're alive." She flung her arms around him again, sobbing.

Which was why Jane wasn't sure she heard what she did.

There was noise all around them. The roar of the fire, the din of the firefighters as they fought the flames for possession of the restaurant. The voices of the paramedics as they were attending to the fire's survivors, not to mention the noise coming from the onlookers who had gathered behind the barricades.

Everything conspired to play a trick on her ears because she could have sworn she heard Jorge say, "I love you."

But she knew that was impossible. That went beyond wishful thinking. That came under the heading of hallucinations.

Until she heard it again.

And then a third time.

Lifting her head, Jane looked at him, stunned. Bedraggled and covered with soot, he still managed to look incredibly sexy. She saw his lips form the three words a fourth time.

Feeling as if she'd just slipped into some parallel universe of her own design, she could only stare in wonder. "Jorge?"

"I love you," he repeated again, his voice growing stronger. As if to help imprint the words into her brain, he grasped her by her arms. "I didn't realize how much until I thought I was going to die in there. And thought about what I was losing, what I had so stupidly thrown away." His eyes looked deep into her soul. "A chance at real happiness."

Oh, how she wanted to believe him. To clutch the words he was saying to her heart.

But she knew better.

"That's just the adrenaline talking," she told him gently.

For some reason, she felt herself growing calm, as if she was the one in control of the situation. It was up to her to make it right. She wasn't going to hold him to promises made at a time like this. It wouldn't be fair of her.

"No," Jorge insisted with fervor, "it's me talking. For the first time, it's me. And for the first time, I'm not afraid to say it. Because I understand what it means." God, he must sound like a loon to her. "I love you," he repeated for the umpteenth time.

"All I could think of in there was that I was going to die and you wouldn't know how I felt."

"You made it clear how you felt," she reminded him quietly. "The last time we were together." She was going to say that she understood, that men like him couldn't be captured, contained, held to promises that the rest of the world made routinely. But she didn't get the chance.

"That was the coward talking," he told her with feeling. A coughing fit interrupted him for a moment. When he got his breath back, he continued. "I'm not a coward anymore."

"I'll say," Murphy, the firefighter who'd handed his father over to the paramedics said as he came up to Jorge. "If you hadn't saved him, your dad would have died in this fire."

"I guess that makes you a hero," Jane told him with pride, threading her arms around his waist and leaning against him. For now, she was content just to hold on to Jorge and not his words. She knew he'd take them back within a few minutes.

But that was all right. It was enough for her that he was alive.

Chapter Fifteen

"No, no, it is not possible."

The vehement protest was coming from José Mendoza. Bundled in a warm blanket that was draped across his shoulders and sitting on the rear step that led into the back of the ambulance, the senior Mendoza had just pulled off the oxygen mask that the paramedic had placed on him to facilitate his breathing.

The gray-haired fire chief did his best to remain patient in the face of all this emotion coming his way. "Mr. Mendoza," he began again in an even voice, "it only stands to reason—"

The sound of his father's voice momentarily diverted Jorge's attention away from Jane.

But as he headed over to his father to see what was going on, Jorge took hold of Jane's hand, silently indicating that she should come along with him to investigate. What concerned him concerned her, and vice versa.

Now and always, he thought, hoping she would give him the second chance he longed for.

Crossing to his father, he put his hand on the older man's shoulder. He felt his father tense. "What's the matter, Pop?"

José frowned and jerked a thumb at the chief. "The chief thinks that the fire was started by one of the kitchen crew."

"Not on purpose," the chief was quick to point out, although his expression indicated that he wasn't entirely sure about that, either. "But you have to admit that grease fires happen in restaurants, Mr. Mendoza. Especially when there's such a high volume of food being prepared."

"No, no, no," José insisted with even more feeling. "My people are careful. They treat this place like their own kitchen—"

The chief looked as if his point had just been made for him. "Mishaps happen in people's kitchens every day, Mr. Mendoza."

"Not my home," José informed him with dour finality. "There must be another cause for the fire. A faulty connection, something that was not caused by human error."

José was clearly issuing a challenge to the fire chief.

His father was working himself up, Jorge thought, concerned. The old man's heart had been through enough today. This couldn't be good for him.

"Pop, take it easy," Jorge counseled. "Nobody got hurt—"

"Except for Red," the man said mournfully, looking over Jorge's shoulder at what was left of the smoldering building. The fire, miraculously, was almost out. Rather than the beautiful, proud building that had stood there just this morning, there was now a half burnt-out shell, some of which was on the verge of collapse.

All those years, just burned away in an instant.

"We've got insurance for that, Pop," Jorge reminded his father gently. "It'll be rebuilt in time for the wedding reception."

"What wedding reception?" Both José and Jane asked at the same time, their voices blending and echoing one another.

Jorge grinned, his eyes going from his father to his love. "Mine—and Jane's."

The horror in José's face brought on by Red's destruction vanished instantly. Wriggling off the ambulance step, oblivious to the blanket that fell from his shoulders, he hugged first his son and then Jane with effervescent feeling.

"Welcome!" he cried as he held on to her. "Welcome to the family."

Stunned by Jorge's cavalier words, it took Jane a moment to return the older man's embrace. She stared at Jorge over his father's shoulder. What was going on here?

"Did I miss something?" she asked Jorge in complete disbelief the moment she was released from his father's embrace. "When did you ask me to marry you?"

"I didn't," Jorge confessed almost sheepishly. The next second, he was back to his normal upbeat temperament. "I just thought that, well, when two people love each other, that's what they do. They get married."

And as the words came out of his mouth, Jorge suddenly realized that he'd just leapfrogged right over the most important issue, taking it for granted.

What if he was wrong about Jane's feelings?

He peered at her face, a hint of uncertainty in his dark eyes even as he kept his smile in place. It was a matter of projecting confidence, of willing something into existence.

"You do love me, don't you?"

"Yes," Jane allowed, saying the single word slowly as if she were tasting it as it crossed her tongue.

Was she dreaming?

Was she the one who'd inhaled too much smoke, had fallen unconscious and was now floating somewhere between the real and the imagined?

Why else was this most perfect of scenarios happening?

"*Hijo*," José said sharply, a disapproving frown on his face. It was clear he felt that he had failed in the education of his second born. "A woman likes to be asked such things. You cannot take them or their answers for granted."

The fact that he was obviously on her side made Jane smile. She'd never had this kind of support when she was growing up.

Very lightly, she touched his arm with affection. "Mr. Mendoza, I think I'm going to like having you for a father-in-law."

Despite his losses and his near-death experience, barely a quarter of an hour old, José beamed at her. "'Pop,' please," he told Jane. "You must call me 'Pop.'" He turned his dark eyes on his son. "And you must ask her properly." Out of the corner of his eye, Jorge saw the fire chief quietly withdrawing. Thank God the man realized that they had time to discuss the cause of the fire later. Right now, this was a family matter and anyone outside the circle of his family didn't belong.

"Jane." Pausing for a moment, Jorge took her hand in his. His eyes never left hers. "Will you make me the happiest man in the world and do me the honor of becoming my wife?"

"Is this part of the bet, too?" she asked, tongue in cheek.

"This is not a bet," he told her. "It stopped being a bet the second I started talking to you and realized what a rare woman you were. Now, please, will you marry me?"

"Yes, oh yes," she cried, rising on her toes and throwing her arms around his neck.

Jorge sealed the proposal with a prolonged, deep kiss.

"Mr. Mendoza, we have to take you to the

hospital," the tall, wiry paramedic who had attended him was saying. He was attempting to steer the older man into the back of the ambulance.

José shrugged the paramedic's hands from his shoulders. "What hospital?" the older man demanded. "I am fine." Looking at his son and future daughter-in-law with unabashed pride, he beamed. "More than fine. Especially when my Maria hears about this."

As if on cue, his petite, dark-haired wife came elbowing her way through the crowd and rushed up to him. The expression on her face was a mix of fear and anger. Fear at what might have happened and anger at what he'd put her through, through no fault of his own.

There were tears shining in her dark eyes.

"*Dios mio,* you are alive, old man. I knew you were too tough to die."

Some of the tears spilled out as she made her declaration. No mention was made of the fact that she had prayed all the way to the restaurant, terrified of what she might find once she got there.

Maria threw her arms around her husband, holding on to his thin frame for all she was worth. "Don't you ever scare me like that again, do you understand?" she demanded. *"Never."*

"It was not something that I had planned, Maria," José told his wife. He shivered when he thought how close he had come to never seeing his wife's face again. "And I wouldn't be here if it wasn't for Jorge."

"Jorge?" she exclaimed. "Jorge was here?" she asked abruptly, looking around wildly for her son. It hadn't occurred to her that he'd been in danger as well. "Where is he?"

Smiling, José tapped his wife on the shoulder then pointed, turning her attention to the kissing couple on the side of the ambulance.

"He's fine," José assured the woman who made his life worth living each day. "And you, Maria, are going to be gaining that daughter-in-law you have been wanting for so long."

Amazed, Maria gave out a whoop of joy, throwing her arms around her husband's neck and squeezing him with wild abandon.

"Finally!" It was then that she saw what was left of Red. Saw the smoldering remains of the restaurant that had been built up by the sweat of her husband's brow. "Oh, José." That was all she said, but it throbbed with an overwhelming sadness. And then she rallied, as she always did, and her natural resilience took hold. "We will rebuild," Maria announced, "and we'll make it even better than before."

"Of course we will," José agreed, draping his arm across his wife's shoulders, already envisioning what the new, improved Red would look like, a phoenix rising out of the ashes of the old. "We need to have some place for the reception."

Marie beamed, patting her husband's chest with her hand in a comfortable, familiar gesture, the way she'd been doing for the last forty-one-plus years. "Yes, we do."

* * *

The crowds that had gathered around the barricades, composed equally of the concerned and the curious, began to slowly disperse. The fire was contained. It had done all the damage it was going to and was no longer a threat to the surrounding area. There was nothing left to witness except for the tedious details of cleanup.

Two of the people who had been milling around the perimeter of the barricade were Ricky Jamison and Josh Fredericks. Like so many others who had been drawn by the sound of the sirens, they had hung around, spectators at the scene of the fire. Fascinated by the power of the flames even as they cheered on the firefighters in their swift, mighty battle to vanquish them.

But now it looked like it was all over. Nothing remained of the blaze but the acrid smell of smoke and ashes that stubbornly and oppressively hung in the air.

Even as the boys had looked on earlier, it was hard for both of them to imagine that a few short weeks ago, they had been inside, partying.

So much could change in a few minutes, Ricky thought. He was tired of hanging back, of waiting to gather his courage in order to leap into life's pool. He'd already made a first effort.

Something he hadn't told Josh yet. He grinned to himself. Wouldn't Josh be surprised? And Jorge— Jorge would be proud of him, he thought.

Bored, Josh turned away from the barricade. He jerked a thumb to the scene behind him, dismissing it. "C'mon, there's nothing left to see here anymore."

Ricky took one last glance at Jorge, a bit of hero worship in his eyes. Even though he'd taken his first steps in the right direction, he was still envious of the man's prowess.

Ricky turned to Josh. The wind ruffled his blond hair and ran up and down his thin torso. He hunched his shoulders against it. As he spoke, he did his best to sound nonchalant. Yet he could feel his heart speeding up and lodging itself in his throat.

"You know." His voice almost cracked and he lowered it. "I asked Lizzie for a date."

Josh glanced at him. "Lizzie?" He repeated the name as if she hadn't been the topic of more than one conversation between them.

"Yeah, Lizzie Fortune," Ricky said her full name, as if his friend didn't know that the girl was part of his every daytime and nighttime dream. "I've had a thing for her for a while now," he added, avoiding eye contact.

A smirk from Josh would have destroyed him no matter how much of a pep talk he'd given himself. He looked up to Josh and valued the older teen's opinion as only a fourteen-year-old could.

"Jorge told me some moves to use and I used them," he said proudly and then grinned. "They worked. She's going out with me next week."

Josh shoved his hands deep into his pockets and slowly began to walk away from the barricade. "You look very satisfied with yourself," he commented.

Shorter than his friend, Ricky lengthened his stride to keep up, trying to maintain that air of nonchalance that Josh always had. "I am. Who knows, this could be the start of something really big. Lizzie might even fall for me."

In response, Josh said nothing. Instead, he just snorted.

Ricky looked at him, confused. He thought his friend would have been happy for him. He'd cheered Josh on when he'd started going out with Lindsey.

"What's that supposed to mean?" he wanted to know, taking offense.

Josh shook his head. His expression seemed enigmatic and far away.

"Nothing," he said dismissively. "Just be careful what you wish for, that's all," Josh advised. There was a distant look in his young eyes as he added, in a voice that was far older than he was, "Love isn't all it's cracked up to be."

Ricky's brow furrowed as he struggled to make sense of what Josh was saying. Why was he acting like that? Only one answer, he realized. "You and Lindsey having problems?"

Josh looked at him sharply. "I didn't say that."

"Well, what did you say?" Ricky wanted to know. He was confused and disappointed. He thought for sure that his friend would have been happy for him. Instead, Josh looked almost moody. Did he want Lizzie for himself? No, Josh liked Lindsey. They were a couple. Everyone knew that. That was part of what made him feel like an outsider. He wanted to be part of a couple too, like Josh.

"Nothing," Josh said with a careless shrug of his

shoulders. "I hope you and Lizzie have a great time together." He dropped the topic. "C'mon. If you want a ride, I've got to get going."

Ricky looked back over his shoulder at the cluster of people near the ambulance. "I feel I should say something to Jorge."

Josh looked at his friend, puzzled. "You mean about Lizzie?"

"No." What was wrong with Josh? Why wasn't he focusing? "About the fire."

This time it was Josh who looked over his shoulder. And saw Jorge kissing that woman he'd picked up at the New Year's Eve party. The one that Ricky had bet him he couldn't get so fast.

"He's busy, Ricky," Josh pointed out. "You can talk to him some other time." Impatience filtered through his voice as he lengthened his stride. "You coming?"

Ricky picked up his pace to keep up with Josh. "Yeah."

Two of the ambulances had already left. One had the woman Darr had rescued inside. The other had taken the busboy, Juan, to the hospital.

Like the rock he'd always been, José had remained where he was, with his wife and growing circle of friends gathering around him to offer their support and encouragement.

Jorge took the opportunity to draw Jane aside, away from the others. He held her hands in his and looked into her eyes, realizing that he would probably be content to go on doing that for quite some time to come.

But life went on and she had one that she'd left when the fire had broken out. He knew it was selfish of him, but he wanted her to remain right where she was, here with him.

"You have to get back to the school?" Jorge finally asked Jane.

The question nudged reality back into focus. Her eyes widened. ReadingWorks! She'd run out of there without so much as a word of explanation. They were all probably wondering where she was. Even so, she shook her head. Her place right now was here—even if he hadn't asked her to marry him. "No, I think they can get along without me for an afternoon."

"Good," he said, "because I can't." His hands tightened on hers, reflecting his feelings. "I want to spend the rest of my life with you." He'd never really explored what those words meant—and never meant them as much as he did right at this moment.

She laughed softly, shaking her head again. He might mean that now, but she was willing to bet he wouldn't later.

"You'll get bored," she predicted.

There she was wrong, he thought. "No, that's one thing I don't think I'll ever be."

She really wished she could believe that. But there was a small part of her that was a realist. Life with parents who'd offered no encouragement had seen to that. "How can you be so sure?"

He told her the truth and bared his heart to her. He realized he'd never allowed himself to be this vulnerable before. But then, he'd never trusted another woman before the way he did her.

"Because I never loved any of the other women. I love you," he declared simply. And then he grinned wickedly. "You still have that Heidi outfit you wore to the hospital?"

What was he getting at? Was he asking if she intended to continue reading to the children at the hospital? "Yes."

His grin grew broader. "Well, that settles it. I will definitely not get bored." His eyes were shining as he told her, "I've always wanted to see what it feels like to be a goat herder."

And then she caught on. And laughed. "Right. You look just like a Swiss goat herder." She ruffled his hair with affection as she said it. Who would have ever thought she'd get this lucky? To have this gorgeous, sexy man want her in his life?

Jorge leaned into her and whispered in her ear. "Use your imagination."

His warm breath created warm ripples of desire all through her.

"I already am," she answered just before she brought her lips up to his.

Jorge didn't need any more of a hint than that. He'd always considered himself pretty quick on the uptake.

This time was no exception. His lips met hers as his soul gratefully slipped back into the paradise that only she created for him.

* * * * *

*Celebrate 60 years of pure reading pleasure
with Harlequin® Books!*

*Harlequin Romance® is celebrating by
showering you with DIAMOND BRIDES
in February 2009.
Six stories that promise to bring a touch
of sparkle to your life, with diamond proposals
and dazzling weddings, sparkling brides
and gorgeous grooms!*

*Enjoy a sneak peek at Caroline Anderson's
TWO LITTLE MIRACLES,
available February 2009
from Harlequin Romance®*

'I'VE FOUND HER.'

Max froze.

It was what he'd been waiting for since June, but now—now he was almost afraid to voice the question. His heart stalling, he leaned slowly back in his chair and scoured the investigator's face for clues. 'Where?' he asked, and his voice sounded rough and unused, like a rusty hinge.

'In Suffolk. She's living in a cottage.'

Living. His heart crashed back to life, and he sucked in a long, slow breath. All these months he'd feared—

'Is she well?'

'Yes, she's well.'

He had to force himself to ask the next question. 'Alone?'

The man paused. 'No. The cottage belongs to a

man called John Blake. He's working away at the moment, but he comes and goes.'

God. He felt sick. So sick he hardly registered the next few words, but then gradually they sank in. 'She's got *what?*'

'Babies. Twin girls. They're eight months old.'

'Eight—?' he echoed under his breath. 'They must be his.'

He was thinking out loud, but the P.I. heard and corrected him.

'Apparently not. I gather they're hers. She's been there since mid-January last year, and they were born during the summer—June, the woman in the post office thought. She was more than helpful. I think there's been a certain amount of speculation about their relationship.'

He'd just bet there had. God, he was going to kill her. Or Blake. Maybe both of them.

'Of course, looking at the dates, she was presumably pregnant when she left you, so they could be yours, or she could have been having an affair with this Blake character before…'

He glared at the unfortunate P.I. 'Just stick to your job. I can do the math,' he snapped, swallowing the unpalatable possibility that she'd been unfaithful to him before she'd left. 'Where is she? I want the address.'

'It's all in here,' the man said, sliding a large envelope across the desk to him. 'With my invoice.'

'I'll get it seen to. Thank you.'

'If there's anything else you need, Mr Gallagher, any further information—'

'I'll be in touch.'

'The woman in the post office told me Blake was away at the moment, if that helps,' he added quietly, and opened the door.

Max stared down at the envelope, hardly daring to open it, but when the door clicked softly shut behind the P.I., he eased up the flap, tipped it and felt his breath jam in his throat as the photos spilled out over the desk.

Oh, lord, she looked gorgeous. Different, though. It took him a moment to recognise her, because she'd grown her hair, and it was tied back in a ponytail, making her look younger and somehow freer. The blond highlights were gone, and it was back to its natural soft golden-brown, with a little curl in the end of the ponytail that he wanted to thread his finger through and tug, just gently, to draw her back to him.

Crazy. She'd put on a little weight, but it suited her. She looked well and happy and beautiful, but oddly, considering how desperate he'd been for news of her for the past year—one year, three weeks and two days, to be exact—it wasn't only Julia who held his attention after the initial shock. It was the babies sitting side by side in a supermarket trolley. Two identical and absolutely beautiful little girls.

* * * * *

When Max Gallagher hires a P.I. to find his estranged wife, Julia, he discovers she's not alone—she has twin baby girls, and they might be his. Now workaholic Max has just two weeks to prove that he can be a wonderful husband and father to the family he wants to treasure.

Look for TWO LITTLE MIRACLES
by Caroline Anderson,
available February 2009
from Harlequin Romance®

CELEBRATE
60 YEARS
OF PURE READING PLEASURE
WITH **HARLEQUIN**®!

We'll be spotlighting a different series
every month throughout 2009
to celebrate our 60th anniversary.

Look for Harlequin® Romance in February!

**Harlequin® Romance is celebrating by showering
you with Diamond Brides in February 2009.**

Six stories that promise to bring a touch of sparkle to
your life, with diamond proposals and dazzling weddings,
sparkling brides and gorgeous grooms!

Collect all six books in February 2009,
featuring *Two Little Miracles* by Caroline Anderson.

*Look for the Diamond Brides miniseries
in February 2009!*

www.eHarlequin.com   HRBRIDES09

HARLEQUIN® Romance®

This February the Harlequin® Romance series
will feature six Diamond Brides stories featuring
diamond proposals and gorgeous grooms.

Share your dream wedding proposal and you could WIN!

The most romantic entry will win a diamond
necklace and will inspire a proposal in one of
our upcoming Diamond Grooms books in 2010.

In 100 words or less, tell us the most romantic
way that you dream of being proposed to.

For more information, and to enter
the Diamond Brides Proposal contest, please visit
www.DiamondBridesProposal.com

Or mail your entry to us at:

IN THE U.S.: 3010 Walden Ave., P.O. Box 9069, Buffalo, NY 14269-9069
IN CANADA: 225 Duncan Mill Road, Don Mills, ON M3B 3K9

You're invited to join our Tell Harlequin Reader Panel!

By joining our new reader panel you will:

- Receive Harlequin® books—they are FREE and yours to keep with no obligation to purchase anything!
- Participate in fun online surveys
- Exchange opinions and ideas with women just like you
- Have a say in our new book ideas and help us publish the best in women's fiction

In addition, you will have a chance to win great prizes and receive special gifts! See Web site for details. Some conditions apply. Space is limited.

To join, visit us at
www.TellHarlequin.com.

REQUEST YOUR FREE BOOKS!
2 FREE NOVELS PLUS 2 FREE GIFTS!

SPECIAL EDITION®

Life, Love and Family!

YES! Please send me 2 FREE Silhouette Special Edition® novels and my 2 FREE gifts (gifts are worth about $10). After receiving them, if I don't wish to receive any more books, I can return the shipping statement marked "cancel." If I don't cancel, I will receive 6 brand-new novels every month and be billed just $4.24 per book in the U.S. or $4.99 per book in Canada, plus 25¢ shipping and handling per book and applicable taxes, if any*. That's a savings of at least 15% off the cover price! I understand that accepting the 2 free books and gifts places me under no obligation to buy anything. I can always return a shipment and cancel at any time. Even if I never buy another book from Silhouette, the two free books and gifts are mine to keep forever.

235 SDN EEYU 335 SDN EEY6

Name   (PLEASE PRINT)

Address   Apt. #

City   State/Prov.   Zip/Postal Code

Signature (if under 18, a parent or guardian must sign)

Mail to the **Silhouette Reader Service:**
IN U.S.A.: P.O. Box 1867, Buffalo, NY 14240-1867
IN CANADA: P.O. Box 609, Fort Erie, Ontario L2A 5X3

Not valid to current subscribers of Silhouette Special Edition books.

Want to try two free books from another line?
Call 1-800-873-8635 or visit www.morefreebooks.com.

* Terms and prices subject to change without notice. N.Y. residents add applicable sales tax. Canadian residents will be charged applicable provincial taxes and GST. Offer not valid in Quebec. This offer is limited to one order per household. All orders subject to approval. Credit or debit balances in a customer's account(s) may be offset by any other outstanding balance owed by or to the customer. Please allow 4 to 6 weeks for delivery. Offer available while quantities last.

Your Privacy: Silhouette is committed to protecting your privacy. Our Privacy Policy is available online at www.eHarlequin.com or upon request from the Reader Service. From time to time we make our lists of customers available to reputable third parties who may have a product or service of interest to you. If you would prefer we not share your name and address, please check here. ☐

SSE08R

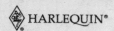

Inside ROMANCE

Stay up-to-date on all your romance reading news!

The Inside Romance newsletter is a FREE quarterly newsletter highlighting our upcoming series releases and promotions!

Click on the <u>Inside Romance</u> link on the front page of **www.eHarlequin.com** or e-mail us at insideromance@harlequin.ca to sign up to receive your FREE newsletter today!

You can also subscribe by writing us at: HARLEQUIN BOOKS
Attention: Customer Service Department
P.O. Box 9057, Buffalo, NY 14269-9057

Please allow 4-6 weeks for delivery of the first issue by mail.

IRNBPA208

COMING NEXT MONTH
Available February 24, 2009

#1957 TRIPLE TROUBLE—Lois Faye Dyer
Fortunes of Texas: Return to Red Rock
Financial analyst Nick Fortune was a whiz at numbers, not diapers.
So after tragedy forced him to assume guardianship of triplets, he
was clueless—until confident Charlene London became their nanny.
That's when Nick fell for Charlene, and the trouble really began!

#1958 TRAVIS'S APPEAL—Marie Ferrarella
Kate's Boys
Shana O'Reilly couldn't deny it—family lawyer Travis Marlowe
had some kind of appeal. But as Travis handled her father's tricky
estate planning, he discovered things weren't what they seemed in the
O'Reilly clan. Would an explosive secret leave Travis and Shana's
budding relationship in tatters?

#1959 A TEXAN ON HER DOORSTEP—Stella Bagwell
Famous Families
More Famous Families from Special Edition! Abandoned by his
mother, shafted by his party-girl ex-wife, cynical Texas lawman
Mac McCleod was over love. Until a chance reunion with his mother
in a hospital, and a choice introduction to her intriguing doctor,
Ileana Murdock, changed everything....

#1960 MARRYING THE VIRGIN NANNY—Teresa Southwick
The Nanny Network
Billionaire Jason Garrett would pay a premium to the Nanny Network
for a caregiver for his infant son, Brady. And luckily, sweet, innocent
nanny Maggie Shepherd instantly bonded with father and son, giving
Jason a priceless new lease on love.

#1961 LULLABY FOR TWO—Karen Rose Smith
The Baby Experts
When Vince Rossi assumed custody of his friend's baby son after an
accident, the little boy was hurt, and if it weren't for Dr. Tessa McGuire,
Vince wouldn't know which end was up. Sure, Tessa was Vince's
ex-wife and they had a rocky history, but as they bonded over the boy,
could it be they had a future—together—too?

#1962 CLAIMING THE RANCHER'S HEART—Cindy Kirk
Footloose Stacie Collins had a knack for matchmaking. After inheriting
her grandma's home in Montana, she and two gal pals decided to
head for the hills and test their theories of love on the locals. When
their "scientific" survey yielded Josh Collins as Stacie's ideal beau, it
must have been a computer error—or was this rugged rancher really a
perfect match?

SSECNMBPA0209